TEN GREEN BOTTLES

AUDREY THOMAS

Design: Michael Macklem. Cover courtesy Margot Ariss.

ISBN 0 88750 215 6 (hardcover)
ISBN 0 88750 216 4 (softcover)

Printed in Canada

PUBLISHED IN CANADA BY OBERON PRESS

IF ONE GREEN BOTTLE...

When fleeing, one should never look behind. Orpheus, Lot's wife. . . penalties grotesque and terrible await us all. It does not pay to doubt. . . to turn one's head. . . to rely on the confusion. . . the smoke. . . the fleeing multitudes. . . the satisfaction of the tumbling cities. . . to distract the attention of the gods. Argus-eyed, they wait, he waits. . . the golden chessmen spread upon the table. . . the opponent's move already known, accounted for. . . . Your pawns, so vulnerable. . . advancing with such care (if you step on a crack, then you'll break your mother's back). Already the monstrous hand trembles in anticipation. . . the thick lips twitch with suppressed laughter. . . then pawn, knight, castle, queen scooped up and tossed aside. "Check," and (click click) "check. . . mmmate." The game is over, and you. . . surprised (but why?). . . petulant. . . your nose still raw from the cold . . . your galoshes not yet dried. . . really, it's indecent. . . inhumane (why bother to come? answer: the bother of not coming). . . and not even the offer of a sandwich or a cup of tea. . . discouraging. . . disgusting. The great mouth opens . . . like a whale really. . . he strains you, one more bit of plankton, through his teeth (my mother had an ivory comb once). "Next week. . . ? At the same time. . . ? No, no, not at all. I do not find it boring in the least. . . . Each time a great improvement. Why, soon," the huge lips tremble violently, "ha, ha, you'll be beating me." Lies. . . all lies. Yet,

5

even as you go, echoes of Olympian laughter in your ears, you know you will return, will once more challenge. . . and be defeated once again. Even plankton have to make a protest. . . a stand. . . what else can one do? "Besides, it passes the time. . . keeps my hand in. . . and you never know. . . . One time, perhaps. . . a slip. . . a flutter of the eyelids. . . . Even the gods grow old."

The tropical fan, three-bladed, omniscient, omnipotent, inexorable, churns up dust and mosquitoes, the damp smell of coming rain, the overripe smell of vegetation, of charcoal fires, of human excrement, of fear. . . blown in through the open window, blown up from the walls and the floor. All is caught in the fan's embrace, the efficient arms of the unmoved mover. The deus in the machina, my old chum the chess-player, refuses to descend. . . yet watches. Soon they will let down the nets and we will lie in the darkness, in our gauze houses, like so many lumps of cheese. . . protected. . . revealed. The night-fliers, dirty urchins, will press their noses at my windows and lick their hairy lips in hunger. . . in frustration. Can they differentiate, I wonder, between the blood of my neighbour and mine? Are there aesthetes among the insects who will touch only the soft parts. . . between the thighs. . . under the armpits. . . along the inner arm? Are there vintages and connoisseurs? I don't like the nights here: that is why I wanted it over before the night. One of the reasons. If I am asleep I do not know who feeds on me, who has found the infinitesimal rip and invited his neighbours in. Besides, he promised it would be over before the night. And one listens, doesn't one? . . . one always believes. . . absurd to rely on verbal consolation. . . clichés so worn they feel like old coins. . . smooth. . . slightly oily to the touch. . . faceless.

Pain, the word, I mean, derived (not according to Skeat) from "pay" and "Cain." How can there, then, be an exit. . .

6

a way out? The darker the night, the clearer the mark on the forehead. . . the brighter the blind man's cane at the crossing. . . the louder the sound of footsteps somewhere behind. Darkness heightens the absurd sense of "situation". . . gives the audience its kicks. But tonight. . . really. . . All Souls'. . . it's too ridiculous. . . . Somebody goofed. The author has gone too far; the absurdity lies in one banana skin, not two or three. After one, it becomes too painful. . . too involved. . . too much like home. Somebody will have to pay for this. . . the reviews. . . tomorrow. . . all will be most severe. The actors will sulk over their morning cup of coffee. . . the angel will beat his double breast above the empty pocketbook. . . the director will shout and stamp his feet. . . . The whole thing should have been revised. . . rewritten. . . we knew it from the first.

(This is the house that Jack built. This is the cat that killed the rat that lived in the house that Jack built. We are the maidens all shaven and shorn, that milked the cow with the crumpled horn. . . that loved in the hearse that Joke built. Excuse me, please, was this the Joke that killed the giant or the Jack who tumbled down. . . who broke his crown? Crown him with many crowns, the lamb upon his throne. He tumbled too. . . it's inevitable. . . . It all, in the end, comes back to the nursery. . . . Jill, Humpty Dumpty, Rock-a-bye baby. . . they-kiss-you, they-kiss-you. . . they all fall down. The nurses in the corner playing Ludo. . . centurions dicing. We are all betrayed by Cock-a-Doodle-Doo. . . . We all fall down. Why, then, should I be exempt?. . . presumptuous of me. . . please forgive.)

Edges of pain. Watch it, now, the tide is beginning to turn. Like a cautious bather, stick in one toe. . . both feet. . . "brr" . . . the impact of the ocean. . . the solidity of the thing, now that you've finally got under. . . like swimming in an ice

cube really. "Yes, I'm coming. Wait for me." The shock of
the total immersion. . . the pain breaking over the head.
Don't cry out. . . hold your breath. . . so. "Not so bad, really,
when one gets used to it." That's it. . . just the right tone. . .
the brave swimmer. . . . Now wave a gay hand toward the
shore. Don't let them know. . . the indignities. . . the chattering teeth. . . the blue lips. . . the sense of isolation. . . . Good.

And Mary, how did she take it, I wonder, the original, the
appalling announcement. . . the burden thrust upon her?
"No, really some other time. . . the spring planting. . . my
aged mother. . . quite impossible. Very good of you to think
of me, of course, but I couldn't take it on. Perhaps you'd call
in again next year." (Dismiss him firmly. . . quickly, while
there's still time. Don't let him get both feet in the door. Be
firm and final. "No, I'm sorry, I never accept free gifts.")
And then the growing awareness, the anger showing quick
and hot under the warm brown of the cheeks. The voice. . .
like oil. . . . "I'm afraid I didn't make myself clear." (Like
the detective novels. . . . "Allow me to present my card. . .
my credentials." The shock of recognition. . . the horror.
"Oh, I see. . . . Yes. . . well, if it's like that. . . . Come this
way." A gesture of resignation. She allows herself one sigh
. . . the ghost of a smile.) But no, it's all wrong. Mary. . .
peasant girl. . . quite a different reaction implied. Dumb-
founded. . . remember Zachary. A shocked silence. . . the
rough fingers twisting together like snakes. . . awe. . . a certain rough pride ("Wait until I tell the other girls. The well
. . . tomorrow morning. . . . I won't be proud about it, not
really. But it is an honour. What will Mother say?") *Droit
de seigneur*. . . the servant summoned to the bedchamber. . .
honoured. . . afraid. Or perhaps like Leda. No preliminaries
. . . no thoughts at all. Too stupid. . . too frightened. . . the
thing was, after all, over so quickly. That's it. . . stupidity. . .
the necessary attribute. I can hear him now. "That girl. . .

8

whatzername? . . . Mary. Mary will do. Must be a simple woman. . . . That's where we made our first mistake. Eve too voluptuous. . . too intelligent. . . this time nothing must go wrong."

And the days were accomplished. Unfair to gloss that over. . . to make so little of the waiting. . . the months. . . the hours. They make no mention of the hours; but of course, men wrote it down. How were they to know? After the immaculate conception, after the long and dreadful journey, after the refusal at the inn. . . came the maculate delivery . . . the manger. And all that noise. . . cattle lowing (and doing other things besides). . . angels blaring away. . . the eerie light. No peace. . . no chance for sleep. . . for rest between the pains. . . for time to think. . . to gather courage. Yet why should she be afraid. . . downhearted. . . ? Hadn't she had a sign. . . the voice. . . the presence of the star? (And notice well, they never told her about the other thing. . . the third act.) It probably seemed worth it at the time. . . the stench. . . the noise. . . the pain.

Robert the Bruce. . . Constantine. . . Noah. The spider. . . the flaming cross. . . the olive branch. . . . With these signs . . . . I would be content with something far more simple. A breath of wind on the cheek. . . the almost imperceptible movement of a curtain. . . a single flash of lightning. Courage consists, perhaps, in the ability to recognize signs. . . the symbolism of the spider. But for me. . . tonight. . . what is there? The sound of far-off thunder. . . the smell of the coming rain which will wet, but not refresh. . . that tropical fan. The curtain moves. . . yes, I will allow you that. But for me . . . tonight. . . there is only a rat behind the arras. Jack's rat. This time there is no exit. . . no way out or up.

(You are not amused by my abstract speculations? Listen . . . I have more. Time. Time is an awareness, either forward or backward, of Then, as opposed to Now. . .the stasis. Time

9

is the moment between thunder and lightning. . . the interval at the street corner when the light is amber, neither red nor green, but shift gears, look both ways. . . the oasis of pleasure between pains. . . the space between the darkness and the dawn. . . the conversations between courses. . . the fear in the final stroke of twelve. . . the nervous fumbling with cloth and buttons, before the longed-for contact of the flesh. . . the ringing telephone. . . the solitary coffee cup. . . the oasis of pleasure between pains. Time. . . and time again.)

That time when I was eleven and at Scout camp. . . marching in a dusky serpentine to the fire tower. . . the hearty counselors with sun-streaked hair and muscular thighs. . . enjoying themselves, enjoying ourselves. . . the long hike almost over. "Ten green bottles standing on the wall. Ten green bottles standing on the wall. If one green bottle. . . should accidentally fall, there'd be nine green bottles standing on the wall." And that night. . . after pigs in blankets . . . cocoa. . . campfire songs. . . the older girls taught us how to faint. . . to hold our breath and count to 30. . . then blow upon our thumbs. Gazing up at the stars. . . the sudden sinking back into warmth and darkness. . . the recovery. . . the fresh attempt. . . delicious. In the morning we climbed the fire tower (and I, afraid to look down or up, climbing blindly, relying on my sense of touch), reached the safety of the little room on top. We peered out the windows at the little world below. . . and found six baby mice, all dead. . . curled up, like dust kitties in the kitchen drawer. "How long d'you suppose they've been there?" "Too long. Ugh." "Throw them away." "Put them back where you found them." Disturbed. . . distressed. . . the pleasure marred. "Let's toss them down on Rachel. She was too scared to climb the tower. Baby." "Yes, let's toss them down. She ought to be paid back." (Everything all right now. . . the day saved. Ararat. . . Areopagus. . . .) Giggling, invulnerable, we hurled the small bodies out the window at the Lilliputian form below. Were we punished? Curious. . . I can't remember. And yet the rest. . . so vivid. . . as though it were yesterday. . . this morning. . . five minutes ago. . . . We must have been punished. Surely they wouldn't let us get away with that?

Waves of pain now. . . positive whitecaps. . . breakers. . . . Useless to try to remember. . . to look behind. . . to think. Swim for shore. Ignore the ringing in the ears. . . the eyes half blind with water. . . the waves breaking over the head. Just keep swimming. . . keep moving forward. . . rely on instinct. . . your sense of direction. . . don't look back or forward. . . there isn't time for foolish speculation. . . . See? Flung up. . . at last. . . exhausted, but on the shore. Flotsam . . . jetsam. . . but there, you made it. Lie still.

The expected disaster is always the worst. One waits for it. . . is obsessed by it. . . it nibbles at the consciousness. Jack's rat. Far better the screech of brakes. . . the quick embrace of steel and shattered glass. . . or the sudden stumble from the wall. One is prepared through being unprepared. A few thumps of the old heart. . . like a brief flourish of announcing trumpets. . . a roll of drums. . . and then nothing. This way. . . tonight. . . I wait for the crouching darkness like a child waiting for that movement from the shadows in the corner of the bedroom. It's all wrong. . . unfair. . . there ought to be a law. . . . One can keep up only a given number of chins. . . one keeps silent only a given number of hours. After that, the final humiliation. . . the loss of self-control . . . the oozing out upon the pavement. Dumpty-like, one refuses (or is unable?) to be reintegrated. . . whimpers for morphia and oblivion. . . shouts and tears her hair. . . . That must not happen. . . . Undignified. . . déclassé. I shall talk to my friend the fan. . . gossip with the night-fliers. . . pit my small light against the darkness, a miner descending the shaft. I have seen the opening gambit. . . am aware of the game's inevitable conclusion. What does it matter? I shall leap over the net. . . extend my hand. . . murmur, "Well done," and walk away, stiff-backed and shoulders high. I will drink the hemlock gaily. . . I will sing. Ten green bottles standing on the wall. If one green bottle should accidentally fall. . . . When it is over I will sit up and call for tea. . . ignore the covered basin. . . the bloody sheets (but what do they do with it afterward. . . where will they take it? I have no experience in these matters). They will learn that the death of a part is not the death of the whole. The tables will be turned. . . and overturned. The shield of Achilles will compensate for his heel.

And yet, were we as ignorant as all that. . . as naïve. . . that we never wondered where the bottles came from? I never wondered. . . . I accepted them the way a small child draws the Christmas turkey. . . brings the turkey home. . . pins it on the playroom wall. . . and then sits down to eat. One simply doesn't connect. Yet there they were. . . lined up on the laboratory wall. . . half-formed, some of them. . . the tiny vestigial tails of the smallest. . . like corpses of still-born kittens. . . or baby mice. Did we think that they had been like that always. . . swimming forever in their little formaldehyde baths. . . ships in bottles. . . snowstorms in glass paperweights? The professor's voice. . . droning like a complacent bee. . . tapping his stick against each fragile glass shell. . . cross-pollinating facts with facts. . . our pencils racing over the paper. We accepted it all without question . . . even went up afterward for a closer look. . . boldly. . . without hesitation. It was all so simple. . . so uncomplex. . . so scientific. Stupidity, the necessary attribute. And once we dissected a guinea pig, only to discover that she had been pregnant. . . tiny little guinea pigs inside. We. . . like children presented with one of those Russian dolls. . . were delighted. . . gratified. We had received a bonus. . . a free gift.

Will they do that to part of me? How out of place it will look, bottled with the others. . . standing on the laboratory wall. Will the black professor. . . the brown-eyed students . . . bend their delighted eyes upon this bonus, this free gift? (White. 24 weeks. Female. . . or male.) But perhaps black babies are white. . . or pink. . . to begin. It is an interesting problem. . . one which could be pursued. . . speculated upon. I must ask someone. If black babies are not black before they are born, at what stage does the dark hand of heredity . . . of race. . . touch their small bodies? At the moment of birth perhaps? . . . like silver exposed to the air. But remember their palms. . . the soles of their feet. It's an interesting problem. And remember the beggar outside the central post office. . . the terrible burned place on his arm. . . the new skin. . . translucent. . . almost a shell pink. I turned away in disgust. . . wincing at the shared memory of scalding liquid . . . the pain. But really. . . in retrospect. . . it was beautiful. That pink skin. . . that delicate. . . Turneresque tint. . . apple blossoms against dark branches.

That's it. . . just the right tone. . . . Abstract speculation on birth. . . on death. . . on human suffering in general. Remember only the delicate tint. . . sunset against a dark sky . . . the pleasure of the Guernica. It's so simple, really. . . all a question of organization. . . of aesthetics. One can so easily escape the unpleasantness. . . the shock of recognition. Cleopatra in her robes. . . her crown. . . . "I have immortal longings in me." No fear. . . the asp suckles peacefully and unreproved. . . . She wins. . . and Caesar loses. Better than Falstaff babbling "of green fields." One needs the transcendentalism of the tragic hero. Forget the old man. . . pathetic . . . deserted. . . broken. The grey iniquity. It's all a question of organization. . . of aesthetics. . . of tone. Brooke, for example. "In that rich earth a richer dust concealed. . . ." Terrified out of his wits, of course, but still organizing, still posturing.

(The pain is really quite bad now. . . you will excuse me for a moment? I'll be back. I must not think for a moment . . . must not struggle. . . must let myself be carried over the crest of the wave. . . face downward. . . buoyant. . . a badge of seaweed across the shoulder. It's easier this way. . . not to think. . . not to struggle. . . . It's quicker. . . it's more humane.)

Still posturing. See the clown. . . advancing slowly across the platform. . . dragging the heavy rope. . . . Grunts. . . strains. . . the audience shivering with delight. Then the last . . . the desperate. . . tug. And what revealed? . . . a carrot. . . a bunch of grapes. . . a small dog. . . nothing. The audience in tears. . . . "Oh, God. . . how funny. . . . One knows, of course. . . all the time. And yet it never fails to amuse. . . I never fail to be taken in." Smothered giggles in the darkened taxi. . . the deserted streets. . . . "Oh, God, how amusing . . . . Did you see? The carrot. . . the bunch of grapes. . . the small dog. . . nothing. All a masquerade. . . a charade. . . the rouge. . . the powder. . . the false hair of an old woman. . . a clown." Babbling of green fields.

Once, when I was ten, I sat on a damp rock and watched my father fishing. Quiet. . . on a damp rock. . . I watched the flapping gills. . . the frenzied tail. . . the gasps for air. . . the refusal to accept the hook's reality. Rainbow body swinging through the air. . . the silver drops. . . like tears. Watching quietly from the haven of my damp rock, I saw my father struggle with the fish. . . the chased and beaten silver body. "Papa, let it go, Papa. . . please!" My father. . . annoyed. . . astonished. . . his communion disrupted. . . his chalice overturned. . . his paten trampled underfoot. He let it go. . . un-

14

hooked it carelessly and tossed it lightly toward the centre of the pool. After all, what did it matter. . . to please the child. . . and the damage already done. No recriminations . . . only, perhaps (we never spoke of it), a certain loss of faith. . . a fall, however imperceptible. . . from grace?

The pain is harder now. . . more frequent. . . more intense. Don't think of it. . . ignore it. . . let it come. The symphony rises to its climax. No more andante. . . no more moderato . . . clashing cymbals. . . blaring horns. . . . Lean forward in your seat. . . excited. . . intense. . . a shiver of fear. . . of anticipation. The conductor. . . a wild thing. . . a clockwork toy gone mad. . . . Arms flailing. . . body arched. . . head swinging loosely. . . dum de dum de DUM DUM DUM. The orchestra. . . the audience. . . all bewitched. . . heads nodding . . . fingers moving, yes, oh, yes. . . the orgasm of sound. . . the straining. . . letting go. An ecstasy. . . a crescendo. . . a coda. . . it's over. "Whew." "Terrific." (Wiping the sweat from their eyes.) Smiling. . . self-conscious. . . a bit embarrassed now. . . . "Funny how you can get all worked up over a bit of music." Get back to the formalities. . . . Get off the slippery sand. . . onto the warm, safe planks of conversation. "Would you like a coffee. . . a drink. . . an ice?" The oasis of pleasure between pains. For me, too, it will soon be over . . . and for you.

Noah on Ararat. . . high and dry. . . sends out the dove to see if it is over. Waiting anxiously. . . the dove returning with the sign. Smug now. . . self-satisfied. . . know-it-all. . . . All those drowned neighbours. . . all those doubting Thomases. . . gone. . . washed away. . . full fathoms five. . . . And he, safe. . . the animals pawing restlessly, scenting freedom after their long confinement. . . smelling the rich smell of spring. . . of tender shoots. Victory. . . triumph. . . the chosen ones. Start again. . . make the world safe for democracy. . . cleansing. . . purging. . . Guernica. . . Auschwitz. . . God's fine Italian hand. Always the moral. . . the little tag. . . the cautionary tale. Willie in one of his bright new sashes/fell in the fire and was burnt to ashes. . . . Suffering is good for the soul. . . the effects on the body are not to be considered. Fire and rain. . . cleansing. . . purging. . . tempering the steel. Not much longer now. . . and soon they will let down the nets. (He promised it would be over before the dark. I do not like the dark here. Forgive me if I've mentioned this before.) We will sing to keep our courage up. Ten green bottles standing on the wall. Ten green bottles standing on the wall. If one green bottle. . . .

The retreat from Russia. . . feet bleeding on the white snow. . . tired. . . discouraged. . . what was it all about anyway? . . . we weren't prepared. Yet we go on. . . feet bleeding on the white snow. . . dreaming of warmth. . . smooth arms and golden hair. . . a glass of kvass. We'll get there yet. (But will we ever be the same?) A phoenix. . . never refusing. . . flying true and straight. . . into the fire and out. Plunge downward now. . . a few more minutes. . . spread your wings. . . the moment has come. . . the fire blazes. . . the priest is ready. . . the worshippers are waiting. The battle over. . . the death within expelled. . . cast out. . . the long hike over. . . Ararat. Sleep now. . . and rise again from the dying fire. . . the ashes. It's over. . . eyes heavy. . . body broken but relaxed. All over. We made it, you and I. . . . It's all, is it not. . . a question of organization. . . of tone? Yet one would have been grateful. . . at the last. . . for a reason . . . an explanation. . . a sign. A spider. . . a flaming cross. . . a carrot. . . a bunch of grapes. . . a small dog. Not this nothing.

STILL LIFE WITH FLOWERS

He has been dead, then, for two days. Yet two days ago, and remembering to allow for the time change, no star fell, no lightning flashed, no premonition ruffled the hairs on the nape of the neck. Two days ago, at the moment, approximately (for those who were there are not prepared to speak), and always allowing for the change in time, what was she doing, what thinking, what? Laying the breakfast table for the following day, knives on one side, forks on the other, neatly, and with a certain—how shall I say—aesthetic satisfaction... or smiling down at the sleeping child, covers flung back and face flushed with the conquests of the morrow... or taking a bath, dissolved in contemplation of a good book waiting on the bedside table? If, as they do with witnesses, she were asked to account for her movements, to be precise, what would I say? How accurate would I be? Did she glance at the kitchen clock, lazily, as she laid the table? Did she register, in any part of her mind (or in the fatigue of her body), the fact that, as she put the last fork in its proper place, the time was ten minutes past ten... the approximate time, allowing for the change, at which he died (though she did not know that yet and he lived on, as it were, for her, until just now and the ringing telephone). Women are neither sailors nor explorers; yet she moves through the days sure-footed, rarely ruffled, hardly glancing at the clock, efficient, automatic, no need for the sun or a compass. When one task is ended another begins, each in its proper order, the way we go round the mulberry bush. We learn early, through mime and imitation, the value of an orderly existence. But now, this. . . this reported disaster. . . the voice on the other end of the phone—heavy, apologetic. "Tomorrow morning. . . . Some of us are going together. . . . Can we offer you a lift?" And what if I refuse to be involved. . . tell me, who will know the difference, or knowing, care? A few flowers. . . a simple card. . . "With deepest sympathy." Adequate. . . reserved. . . the proper thing to do. And still the day would not be interrupted. . .overturned. And if I go, the problems. . . the rushing about. . . the phone call to the sitter. It is late now. She is probably asleep, or if awake, won't want to come out in the daytime. . . take the bus. . . has something else to do. She too must be disturbed. . . her friendship put upon. Why bother? Besides. . . I do not like this sort of thing, this cinematic show of grief, these public gestures. Tokens. What comfort can they possibly supply. . . to him. . . to her. . . to anyone? I'm afraid.

When she was in the sixth grade the teacher—her name escapes me—died of cancer. And the principal (now dead himself?) decided they should all go to the funeral, en masse, suitably chaperoned, in Sunday suits and dresses, to pay their last respects (or first, for we hadn't liked her). Each child would throw a single rose. . . how sweet. . . into the open casket, as they all filed by. I did not like the teacher, who was, or had been, very fat, and wore a grey puff of hair in each nostril, as though she were in the habit of sniffing ancient dandelions. She read us poems. . . this was during the war. . . of soldiers lying in forgotten fields, of orphan children wailing in the Blitz. And as she read she wept. . . great oily tears. . . which left their tracks behind them on her powdered face, like snails. And as she read she sat. . . legs crossed above the knee. . . the brown tourniquets

18

of her rolled stockings clinging to her fat thighs. I used to wonder what would happen if they broke, if that tremendous load of fat, upon release of pressure, would suddenly fall down and the teacher trickle away in oily drops upon the shiny shoe-worn classroom floor. She had not come back after Christmas. . . and I was glad. . . as were the rest of us, I think. Spring came and we forgot her.

But then they made us go to the funeral home. . . en masse. . . after the principal had held a special solemn meeting of the PTA. They decided we were old enough to cope with death. . . the sixth grade. . . and besides, it would be such a pretty gesture. The children wouldn't stay, of course, to see the casket closed. They'd leave before the graver parts. It would all be over so quickly. . . and mean so much to the old woman who had given forty years. . . the best years of her life. . . to children, to the moral education of young minds. The rest of the day would be declared a holiday. When it was her turn to pass the casket, brown and shiny like the gaberdine skirt the teacher had worn, winter and summer, for many years, she tried to avert her eyes and walk quickly. . . to hold her breath and not inhale the dreadful, dreadful odour of gardenias. . . of furniture polish, dust and grief. Tried to shut out the sound of someone sobbing in the front row of chairs. . . the knowledge that the principal was watching. . . the organist waiting with his hands poised over the yellow keys. Yet she could not help herself . . . looked down. . . as from a great and dizzying height. . . and saw the wax face of her teacher. . . the tiny puffs of hair . . . the tired face fixed in a grotesque and eternal smile, as though she knew a dreadful secret. Unable to breathe, to listen to that broken sound of sobbing, ragged and dangerous as broken glass, she stumbled out of line. . . dry-eyed and terror-struck. . . out of the musty building. . . into the warm spring afternoon. It was only when she was outside in the street, staring blankly at the huge and goat-like face of Uncle Sam, his finger to his lips, and underneath the warning—"Shh. The Enemy Might Be Listening!" that she realized she was still holding her rose. . . the rose intended for her teacher. . . in her hand. She ran all the way home and buried the rose in the garden, wondering if the teacher would somehow get a message to the principal.

That night I dreamt of my dead teacher. . . in a top hat of red, white and blue. . . pointing me out in Assembly as the Enemy. . . the principal and all the other children running after me, pelting me with roses. But there were no reprisals, except some teasing from the other children. And I never really thought of her again, until today. Except once, on Hallowe'en. . . a children's party. Wearing my flame-proof costume I had gone early, trick-or-treating from door to door. Sometimes sticky sweets, and sometimes apples. Once in a while, from the big houses on the Drive, a penny. And afterwards the party. . . in someone's barn. We played a children's game called Dead Man's Body. In the dark, giggling, we passed around a glove filled with cold porridge . . . the dead man's hand. . . peeled grapes for eyeballs. . . a plate of cold spaghetti for his guts. I was afraid—a big girl like me—but was persuaded to stay and bob for apples. I had thought I felt the dead hand of my teacher. And after that I never attended another funeral. A multitude of aunts, uncles, cousins—even my grandmother—all had been laid to rest while I was at home with whatever ailment, or excuse, I had been able to conjure up at the time. Did anyone ever suspect that it was the memory of a buried rose. . . a wax face. . . that kept me away? If so, it was never mentioned, or not in my presence. Never talked about.

Since that day she had never gazed upon the face of death . . . and now she was afraid. . . but why? The casket. . . surely . . . will be closed. Console yourself with the thought that he, at least, will not be subjected to the humiliation of the cosmetician's palette, will not be made up for an appointment already, and so disastrously, kept. The idea of gazing at him while he is unaware of her gaze. . . surely that is repugnant to her? Wasn't she always uncomfortable, slightly ashamed, when, as a child, she awoke too early. . . tiptoed into her parents' room where they were both still sleeping . . . and she was left alone. . . somehow an intruder. . . in a room to which they, as conscious beings. . . had not yet returned? Wasn't she always slightly afraid to wake them. . . as though she wondered if, in fact, they were really there?

It is only this one time. . . a matter of getting in a car. . . of making a token gesture. . . and one can always stand well back. There should be many people. He had a lot of friends . . . it's not a question of the solitary mourner. And the washing can be put off for another day. . . or taken to the laundromat. . . or done when she returns.

Now, as we ride in a strange car, through the streets of a city somehow suddenly foreign, past raucous billboards and other cars and hurrying figures which seem to bob and float in the fog, I wonder sadly why she bothered to come at all. The others in the car she does not know, or only as his friends. They seem incomplete and uninteresting, like a group picture with the central figure hidden or cut out. They talk together in low tones, their very voices pallid in the grey air of this important morning. They do not speak to her. . . the others. . . or seem to notice her presence at all. As though to reassure herself of her existence she feels an overwhelming desire to ask a question. . . make a comment . . . but what to ask and what to comment on? The question dies in her throat and she sits miserable, nursing her bitterness and fear and grief like the uninvited guest at a party who stands awkwardly with a stale drink, swirling the brown liquid at the bottom of the glass. Waiting for the miracle which will whisk him safely back to the warm solitude of his own room. Glancing at his watch, wondering how long before he can safely leave. Cursing the man who suggested he come along.

The car crosses the bridge to the other side of the city and moves slowly toward the mountains, leaving a trail of wet marks behind it like that of a small brown snail. The fog is so heavy that the mountain tops are hidden, but she knows that they are there and this is somehow reassuring. When they reach the cemetery they discover they are early, have to wait, and an old man in a yellow oilskin directs them toward a queue of waiting cars. Therefore, it is not the same as at a wedding. They do not ask if we are friends of the bride, or of the groom. The dead are sexless; they are only the dead, and there can be no distinction except between them and the living. The old man in his oilskin. . . it is right to say, because of age, of seniority. . . that he is closer to the dead than I am? A question of semantics really. . . what do we mean by closer? At any rate, he does not mind his job. . . seems to enjoy his position. . . the garish authority of his yellow coat. . . hurries now from car to car, whispering some order or request through the slit of window hastily turned down. Now he reaches our car. . . crouches down. . . his breath sends moist signals of reassurance through the open window. . . his bird's-egg eyes are twinkling with importance. (How many burials here a day. . . a week. . . a month? Does he get paid for piecework, like a seamstress? Do we tip him, in the end?) "Wait in the car until the hearse arrives, folks. No need to get pneumonia standin' in the wet." We all smile feebly, and he swims away.

The young man. . . driver of the car. . . turns the motor off and glances briefly at his watch, as though he were checking the arrival time of train or plane. . . then takes a paper from his briefcase and begins to read. No sound but the sound of people breathing. . . softly as though ashamed. . . and the heavy thumps of wind against the roof. . . like clods. We sit in uncomfortable silence. . . four extras waiting in the wings. . . for the cue, the signal that will lead us onto the stage, for the solemn crowd scene at the end. Only the old man seems really alive at all. . . hurries from forth to back again and forth. . . lining up cars and shaking his head, as though pleased at the good "turnout," in spite of the weather, the rain. We sit like figures in a paperweight, waiting to be seized and shaken up. Several cars have driven up behind and when she turns her head she can see vaguely, out of the back window, a vague, familiar bearded face. . . which flashes off and on the other windshield. . . as the wiper moves in rhythm across the window. . . back. . . across again. On. . . off. . . on. . . off. She watches the face with a curious sense of satisfaction, the image drowned. . . in one instant . . . by the mist. . . miraculously coming alive again in the next, under the steel and rubber efficiency of the wiper. . . which cuts across the moisture like a knife. Then when the face does not appear. . . the dripping glass revealing nothing . . . she panics. . . only to realize with relief. . . deducing from the presence of a dim red glow. . . visible near the face when next the wiper swept across the glass. . . that the face had not. . . how stupid. . . been erased. . . but had only, for a moment. . . bent down to light a cigarette. Now she fastens her attention on the glow. . . rather than the face. . . finding here the indication of some warmth, as well as the abstraction of the small red dot. . . a circle with no hollows or protuberances indicating the presence of eyes or mouth (an uninhabited sun), somehow more bearable. But no. The more she concentrated on the dot as circle. . . the more it wavered. . .pushed itself beyond circumference. . . became a ball. . . a flower. . . red like the sun. . . and yet a face. . . like the man in the moon. . . evil. . . fascinating. . . the face of all the night creatures who had hovered round her bed or hid in corners when she was a child. But suddenly. . . the moon descended. . . the red ball broke. . . the flower opened, bloomed into the face of her sixth-grade teacher. . . mouth open. . . eye sockets empty. . . shouting unintelligible obscenities through the wall of safety glass and water. She shudders, turns away.

It's best to think of nothing. . . to be nothing but an actor waiting for his cue. . . a traveller anticipating far-off places . . . the whistle of the train which cuts away the darkness. . . takes me away. . . a child asleep in a metal womb. But her mind. . . like a conscientious housewife who finds she has unexpectedly a "free" morning in which to remain in bed much later than is normal. . . and yet is so used to activity, to keeping busy, that she finds it impossible to lie still. . . a princess lying on the pea of custom. . . her mind refuses to relax, but continues to run its practiced fingers over dusty crevices . . . to open doors long shut. . . to pick up memories and turn them over, as though they were mementos of some long-forgotten holiday, or piles of mending (torn trousers, hanging buttons) in need of repair. The other people in the car, the young man who was driving, his pregnant wife, the older man who sat beside her, began to talk in normal tones, as though the dead man, being late, had forfeited his right to be mourned. Yet as I listen to them, enclosed in the same glass cage, the paperweight of expectation, their talk reveals uneasiness, fear, as we wait in this curious fog-bound twilight between private grief and public gesture of respect. Survivors of a shipwreck, thrown together by fate, by circumstance too horrible to mention, they try to close their eyes to the terrible sight of all those who drowned before they reached the raft. . . reassure one another about their possible chance of being sighted by a ship or a search plane . . . recount grotesque and exaggerated tales of other ship-

24

wrecks and survivors who had undergone incredible hard-ships and had yet managed to survive. . . to "come through all right." But always in the end. . . back to the graver truths . . . the known catastrophes.

"It's hardly safe to cross a street in broad daylight, the way people drive these days."

"And if you aren't knocked down by a car or mugged by some teenager who has a gripe against his parents which he takes out on the back of your head, the chances are that you're going to be blown off the face of the earth by some-body pressing the wrong button. Did you see Dr. Strange-love?" And so they go on, strange formal diction. . . clichés . . . stereo-thoughts. . . like Egyptian slaves toiling across the sands with new chunks of disaster. . . until they have erected a veritable pyramid. . . an awesome monument to sudden death and the uncertainty of survival. Passionless. . . metro-nomic. . . the living.

Yet all those hypothetical deaths are comforting, are they not? Because they always happen. . . or are about to happen . . . to someone we do not know: a name in the papers (or picture sprawled across the morning's headlines). . . a man or a woman, sometimes a child. . . of whom we do not know. His name, which we do know, his death, with which we are all more or less familiar, is never mentioned. And for me, who knew him both best and least, his death is as real and personal as if it were my own. When I put down the phone it was as though, in a leg which had been amputated, there were intense pain where no pain should have been. . . in the leg no longer there. . . a grief of the body. . . an ache of the roots for what once grew and was alive and now would neither grow nor live again. Three days now, has he been dead. . . yet how many times not living because not there? Away so long, it is as though now, and since the news of his death (the news last night—the death three days ago)

25

. . . now the leg has suddenly grown again, and my body. . . having become accustomed to the reality of an unreal pain . . .having grown to welcome it, perhaps (for the existence of the pain was proof, was it not, of the previous existence of the leg?), was unable to readjust. When he went away there was pain. . . and the pain became familiar, desired. . . a kind of medicine, in fact; for where the pain was he was still. Scars of an old wound prove that the battle has, in fact, been fought. Now they have brought him back, it is his presence, not his death, I fear. I will have to walk forever on three legs. . . one of my own and two of his (two of my own and one of his). . . an old woman with a stick. Her mind, filled with the terror of the future, returned to the past. . . wandered along the rocky shore of consciousness. . . picked up stones. . . replaced them carefully. (But not before the creatures underneath had fled. . . escaped from their rocky prison. . . scampered away in the darkness, making a soft moist sound like children whispering together in the dark, or taffeta leaves against a window on a summer night.)

It had begun to rain early that morning as well, and by evening, bored and restless and knowing I would not sleep with the rain relaying secrets to the windows all night long, I had decided to go to the party. Only because of the rain . . . for she did not like large parties. . . unknown people. . . gin in paper cups. . . nowhere to sit but on the steps or floor . . . nothing to say. Not shy, exactly, but incapable of small talk. . . governed by a peculiar respect for words. . . a primitive respect. . . as though each time she uttered a word or phrase, she gave herself. . . or part of herself. . . away. Only because of the rain and not being able to sleep. Alone only because her husband refused to go. . . was tired (why not?) after his long day's work. . . wanted to read a book. "The rain will be good for the garden," my husband had said after dinner. "But I am not a garden," I replied, and went upstairs to put on my gayest dress, my daintiest shoes, to spread my peacock feathers in the face of the rain. . . to compete with the music of the rain. . . to stamp out its message with a silver shoe. . . drown out its message with a silver laugh. He followed her from her bath, stood framed in the doorway as she dressed, smiled at her serious face. "You are very lovely," he had said, "and should not go alone." But he would not come with me. . . so I smiled. . . spread out the feathers of my skirt. . . snapped on a silver bangle. . . and was gone. Was gone and had enjoyed herself. . . how strange. Had smiled and listened and danced, drunk gin from paper cups and sat on steps, not saying much, but smiling. . . re-gretting, when the party began to break up, that the night was nearly over. . . searching rather forlornly for her coat amidst the pile flung, only a minute before, or so it seemed, upon the bed. "You'll catch pneumonia in those shoes," the other said, when she announced her wish to walk home in the rain. He offered her a lift, and she accepted, allowed him who was carless to borrow a car from a friend, a bearded young man whose name she had never known or could not now remember. Slowly and carefully he drove through the streets of the city. . . deserted now. . . and the silence rode between them like a velvet cushion. . . inviting her to rest her head upon it and be still.

"It is as though everyone else were dead," he said at last, "and you and I, here in this borrowed car, the only ones left alive." She smiled at this. . . said nothing. . . only her brace-lets as she smoothed her hair. . . gave a shy little murmur of assent. And suddenly they were parked, not in front of her house. . . but in a street elm-shaded green and silver. . . a fairy world of rain and soft shadows. . . and his voice, like rain, murmuring in her ear please, oh please, I want you now. . . tonight. . . I want you. Feel how warm it is how ready please. . . . And her body. . . alien now. . . a wild and fairy thing of green and silver. . . begotten of the darkness and the silence, called into being by his voice, the sound of the sea in her ear. Her body and her competent hands. . . which ruled her safe and daylight world as surely as the hands upon the clock upon the kitchen wall; her hands, her mouth. . . betrayed her. She knew in her heart that the trees were tearing their sea-green hair, shedding their silver tears, tapping their warning fingers against the window of the car. But she did not choose to hear. Her silver bracelets sang a frenzied tune and then were still while the man, the rain, her body, her peacock dress dissolved in the silver light. . . became one in the darkness of a borrowed car. . . on a deserted street. . . down which she would walk with her child, if it were fine, in the morning. Afterward. . . we covered our nakedness with the hastily gathered leaves of conversation . . . cigarettes (I'm sorry. It won't happen again), and then drove home, the silence, now unwelcome, sitting hunched between us like some huge and hungry beast.

The house was dark. . . lidded. . . unfriendly, as she paused before getting out of the car. "How do I look?" she asked. "Like a frightened child," he answered, reaching across to open the door. "Do you expect a mark, some sign upon your forehead?" (And he kissed her there) "I expect nothing. . . ask for nothing, except. . . somehow. . . to be forgiven." "By him?" and then when she did not answer, "By me?" "By myself." "It won't happen again, I promise you." "Never again."

The hearse. . . a sleek black bird with folded wings. . . turns into the cemetery now, and now the gay yellow arms of the commissionaire go wild as he backs and points, points and backs, until the black car safely taxis down the runway, comes to a stop before the open grave. At the end of the drive a sign. . . suddenly appearing, conjured perhaps from the wide yellow sleeves of the old man. . . just as rabbits and flags and bouquets of paper flowers used to materialize suddenly from magic fingers at the birthday parties of my childhood: QUIET. CEREMONY IN PROGRESS. Black letters on a yellow ground. Doors slammed. Umbrellas, batlike, opened. She and her three companions walked toward the waiting hearse. Is it like a dump truck then? Does the back tip up to slide the coffin down a silver gangplank. . . into a sea of mud? But no. . . four young men. . . self-conscious. . . try not to look afraid. . . step forward from the crowd and raise the heavy coffin, blue as sky, from the back of the hearse, setting it down on something that resembles, to her, a luggage rack. Once, coming back from a holiday abroad, I had been stopped by customs and made to open all my cases, take everything out and heap it on the counter before the officer had silently X'd my luggage and walked away, leaving me red-faced and furious, to sort through rumpled dresses, dirty underwear, and little balls of stockings, and to put everything back in place, while people stared and snickered. Was he put in there like that. . . his broken body. . . his torn face. . . his ragged self. . . stuffed anyhow into a sky-blue coffin. . . the lid slammed quickly down? Had those who placed him there been quick enough to keep out all the darkness. . . all the silence. . . or were they sitting there hunched at his feet as they had sat at hers during the long and rainy autumn nights. . . or walked beside her under the bright blue lid of summer sky?

No hymns. . . no long orations. . . it is over. The crowd moves away, back to the safety of their cars, their throbbing engines. . . quickening their pace a little in anticipation of a hot lunch and a welcome change of shoes. She stands there for a moment. . . alone. . . with eyes uplifted. . . staring into the white-faced, dark-haired girl across the grave. Their eyes meet briefly. . . flicker together like struck matches. . . across the dull gulf of grave and falling rain. She can see the spray

29

of flowers. . . their delicate red lips soon to close now open . . . to the wet caress of sky. . . nestled as if for shelter among the large and more elaborate offerings on the grave. Swiftly and without speaking she kneels down. . . and plucks a single flower from the centre of the spray. Twisting it in her wet hair she walked back slowly. . . to her prison and her open-mouthed companions in the waiting car.

XANADU

In the beginning it was hardly paradise. That first night, "the night of the dreadful overture," as she was to call it later, when they had arrived at last at the house, bones aching from the long drive up from the harbour (over a road so pock-marked with holes it looked, as her husband said, "as though an army had blown it up as they retreated"), heads reeling from that first sensuous shock which Africa invariably delivers to the European consciousness, only to discover that the house was in utter darkness and the steward who had been engaged for them by the university was dead drunk on the front verandah (had quite literally stumbled upon this last discovery and experienced a thrill of horror, thinking, for a moment, that the man was dead, not drunk); when they had solved the mysteries of hanging mosquito nets and sent the children off to bed with the remains of the picnic lunch inside them ("we couldn't find so much as a can opener"); when she had inhaled the general atmosphere of damp and decay (which even two Bufferin tablets and a large whisky failed to dispel), had succumbed to self-pity and despair and anger, as she did the only sensible thing a woman can do in such circumstances —put her head in her hands and wept. "The whole thing seemed a vast conspiracy," she said to her friends later, "and I felt, somehow, that a large and highly organized 'unwelcoming committee' had been at work." Then she would add, with a small laugh at her own idiosyncrasies, "I attach great importance to beginnings, to signs and portents you might say. My Irish ancestry I suppose." What made it worse was the fact that her husband insisted upon treating the whole thing as a joke, an adventure. "Jason seemed to find it all so interesting, so novel. He kept sticking his head out the door and sniffing—like a great dog who wanted to be let out, or a child on his first night of vacation. I honestly think that if I had been the violent sort—" (a pause while she impishly regarded her listeners and smiled the delightful smile which had made her such a favourite with both men and women) "—if I had been the violent sort I would have killed him on the spot. There is nothing more irritating," she would continue in a half-humorous, half-philosophic tone, "than the sight of another person enjoying a situation which you yourself find absolutely intolerable. *He* couldn't wait for daylight because he wanted to explore. *I* couldn't wait for daylight because I wanted to find the way to the nearest travel office."

Yes, it made for an amusing tale, in retrospect, but it could hardly be called an auspicious beginning. The next morning, in spite of the terrible and tiring events of the day before, she awoke early; and being unable to return to sleep or to endure the sight of her husband's peaceful face on the pillow beside her, she dressed quickly and went down to the kitchen. She was surveying with distaste a platoon of small ants who were breakfasting off the dirty dishes of the night before when she heard a light tap, tap ("almost like a discreet cough") on the kitchen door. Thinking it might be someone from the university, someone who would apologize for their not having been met; for their having to arrive in the dark, the pouring rain, alone and helpless; for the drunken steward, the missing can opener, the musty sheets, for the whole initial fiasco, she flung open the door

"as full of righteous indignation as a balloon about to pop."
There on the stoop stood a large black man, the blackest
man she had ever seen. He was clad only in a pair of khaki
shorts and a tattered string vest. She was still in that state,
not at all unusual for a European, when all Africans look
alike; so, although she had seen the steward of the night
before, had seen him clearly in the light of her husband's
torch, she did not realize at first that the two men bore very
little resemblance to one another and she immediately as-
sumed that they were the same. Naturally she was furious,
and she spoke to him very sharply. ("I nearly sent him
away!")

"I thought my husband made it very clear to you last
night that your services would no longer be required. And
if you think you're getting any wages for yesterday's performance you're very much mistaken." He watched her,
impassive yet without hostility, and waited politely until she
had finished. "There was I, screaming at the poor man like
some fishwife, and he never moved a muscle; never even,
as I recall, batted an eye." (Of course she was elaborating
a little here. In actual fact she had never raised her voice,
was furiously calm, spoke slowly and methodically as
though, with each word, she were giving him a sharp but
precise blow from an unseen hammer. But it made a better
story the other way, and she enjoyed the picture she created
in her listeners' minds, enjoyed the implication that she,
who seemed the mildest of women, had been, at the outset,
the typical European bitch. "I was positively archetypal,"
she would cry, and wrinkle her delightful nose with laughter and pretended self-distaste.) Yet when she had finished
her little speech, the man did not go away as she expected
and she spoke to him again. "Well? What is it you want?
You can hardly expect us to give you a reference, can you?"

"No, Madame. Please, Madame, I know nothin' about

yesterday. I have only just arrived. Do you want a steward, Madame?" It was then that she looked at him closely, *really* looked at him, and realized her terrible mistake, her awful blunder.

"I'm terribly sorry," she said, and smiled her brilliant smile—the smile that had endeared her to countless cab-drivers, milkmen and meter-readers (not to mention her wide circle of friends) back home. "I thought you were someone else. Our steward, I mean the steward engaged for us, was drunk when we arrived. We sent him away, and I thought you were he. I've been very rude to you. Forgive me." She found herself offering an apology where no apology had, in fact, been demanded. Perhaps precisely because none had been asked for, not even hinted at in the man's impassive but polite silence; or perhaps because the awareness of centuries of what one might call, euphemistically, European bad manners made her feel that an apology was due and overdue. He accepted the apology in the same way in which he had accepted the accusations—with a polite silence. Yet this very silence seemed to comfort her, seemed to indicate that he understood and approved first, the anger, and second, the apology. But all he did, verbally, was to repeat, "Please, Madame, do you need a steward?"

"Can you cook?" she asked. He could.

"Can you read and write?" He could do this as well. ("Although why I asked that question, then, when all I needed, all I was desperate for, was someone who could clean and scrub and make the wretched stove light, who could bring domestic order out of the chaos into which we had been plunged, I'll never know." She did not remember that she had overheard a woman on the boat say that it was a tremendous advantage if "they" could read and write.)

"Well, then," she said, "you're hired."

"Just like that?" her listeners would ask in wonder and

34

admiration. "Just like that," she would reply with a laugh. "Call it instinct, call it what you will; I somehow felt that he was what we wanted, what we needed, and that it would be ridiculous to ask for letters of reference, or his job book, with all those ants crawling around and the children about to wake up and want their breakfast. It was as though I had rubbed a lamp and the genie had appeared. "One doesn't," she added with a laugh, "ask a genie for his testimonials."

And indeed, it did seem like magic. In minutes the dishes were done, the kitchen swept ("the broom seemed to appear from nowhere") and a large pan of bacon and eggs was frying merrily on the stove. Full of excitement she ran up the stairs which she had descended with such foreboding just half an hour before. She found her husband in the children's room, searching through suitcases for clean underwear and socks, for dry sandals (the eldest had managed to step in a puddle the night before), and a missing Teddy bear. The room was in chaos, and for a moment she experienced a renewal of despair as she glanced at the disorder and the all-too-obvious grime of the room itself. But then she remembered her errand, her news. "Listen, Jason, we've got a steward." "We had a steward, you mean," he replied from the corner, where he was trying to persuade the eldest that one brown sandal and one red would look very gay.

"No," she shook her head slowly, triumphantly, "we've got one—a new one. I just hired him."

"Good," he said. And that was all. No questions were asked—nothing. It seemed to him the most natural thing in the world that a steward should appear out of nowhere, and that his wife should hire him on the spot. She was a little put out, a little irritated, that her announcement did not, somehow, seem worthy of blaring trumpets and waving flags. Something (it couldn't have been spite) made her ask, "What if he isn't any good?"

"He'll be good," said her husband. And he was. By the time they all trooped down to breakfast, the sitting-room had been swept, the ashtrays emptied, and the table laid with an almost military precision. A pot of coffee stood ready (a hot pad placed carefully under it, she noted with approval), a bowl of fruit was waiting at each place, and she settled herself at the head of the table with a shy, triumphant smile—like a soldier modestly returning home, his erect back and grave smile bearing mute witness to battles won and obstacles endured. Everything was delicious: crisp bacon, solid but not solidified eggs, a veritable regiment of toast lined up for their inspection. And all the time the steward was moving to and fro, his sandals slapping efficiently on the terrazzo floor. Plates were whisked away and clean plates substituted; a second rack of toast appeared, more steaming coffee: all this done so quickly, so quietly that the large black man might have been another Ariel with hosts of spirits at his command. The children were delighted, intrigued.

"Did *he* get the breakfast, Mommy? What's his name?" It came as a shock to her, almost as a sensation of good manners breached, that she had, in fact, forgotten to ask him his name. So when he appeared again she turned her shy, brilliant smile on him once more, extended her smile to him, offered it, the way a friend will convey apology with the soft pressure of a hand.

"I'm terribly sorry. I forgot to ask your name."

"Joseph, Madame." And then, a bit confused as to how to end the brief interview (for she had never dealt with servants before), she simply played her smile over his face once more and reached for the marmalade.

By noon, when they had all returned from an exploratory trip around the compound, had met the registrar and gracefully accepted his equally graceful apologies for thinking that their ship was due in on the tenth, not the ninth; had explained to him about the drunken steward and the lack of electricity; had been assured that the man, if he could be found, would be dealt with, and had been informed, again with a graceful apology, that the electricity was always off on Thursday evenings; when they had collected their mail and bought a few things at the little shop, they discovered that the chaos of the bedrooms had disappeared. Suitcases had been unpacked and set out on the upstairs verandah to air, the children's clothes had been carefully sorted and put away, beds had been stripped of their musty sheets and mattresses laid outside to absorb the sun. They discovered Joseph in the bathroom, kneeling over the tub and methodically kneading dirt out of the mosquito nets. Even the missing Teddy bear had been found. And later, after a (by now) predictably delicious lunch, as she lay on her immaculate bed in a state of happy exhaustion and listened to the laughter of the children, who were taking turns on an ancient swing which her husband had discovered at the bottom of the garden, she decided that things had, after all, turned out for the best. She felt, somehow, that she almost owed that miserable creature of the night before a vote of thanks. For if they hadn't had to send him away, then she, in turn, would have sent Joseph away that morning. A bad beginning, she reflected philosophically, just before she dozed off, does not necessarily imply a bad ending.

Thus the days slipped by, each one like some perfect, exotic jewel set carefully and expertly into her golden chalice of contentment. What of mosquitoes? Joseph examined the nets each day, and sprayed the lounge each evening after dinner while they sipped a cup of coffee on the verandah. What of the rains? At the first tentative rumble Joseph ran swiftly through the house, shutting the louvres, bringing in the washing, checking that the candlesticks were ready if the electricity should go off and remain off after dark. What of the orange lady, the bean man, the itinerant traders —the steady stream of merchandise which arrived each day? Joseph took care of it all—made certain that only the biggest oranges at the smallest price, the choicest beans, the largest bunch of bananas, the most serious traders, ever passed her threshold. For the first time in more years than she cared to remember she felt "caught up" with the sheer mass of business necessary to maintaining a comfortable, well-run home. For the first time she could wake up in the morning without a moral hangover, a sense of things left undone or done too hastily, of buttons still missing or unmatched socks. Instead, at six o'clock came the gentle, cough-like knock announcing the arrival of morning tea. Then they dressed, and while her husband shaved and collected the books he would need that morning, she dressed the children for school. By 6.30 breakfast was on the table; by seven her husband had left; by 7.30 the eldest child had been picked up by the little school bus which travelled the compound. She read and played games with the little one until it was 8.15 and his turn to be picked up for nursery school. How strange it seemed, at first, to take her coffee out on the verandah and contemplate the day before her, the day that would unroll like a red carpet under her feet, to choose what she wanted to do, to ignore unmade beds and dirty dishes, washing and ironing, what to serve for lunch. She felt almost as though she were a convalescent who was now recovering slowly but happily, aware perhaps for the first time of the small beauties of the world, the large beauty of being alive at all. Joseph took care of everything—everyone; moved swiftly and noiselessly in and out of their days, a dark brown shuttle weaving a gay-coloured carpet for her delight.

Yet with all this idleness, this new and unaccustomed leisure, she wasn't bored—not for a minute. She embarked, first of all, on a plan of self-improvement, sent away for books which she had always meant to read, decided to brush up on her French, to begin German. "After all," she said to Jason one evening as they sat on the verandah observing the strange, almost embarrassed pink of the tropical sunset, "I may never have this chance again."

"Which chance is that?"

"The chance to spread my intellectual wings a bit, to grow—as a person, I mean."

"Begin," he said with a teasing smile, "by keeping still and watching that sky."

But his teasing never bothered her, and she was perceptive enough to realize that even the most sympathetic of husbands could not possibly understand what it was like to be suddenly released from all the never-ending pressures of housework, the domestic cares that had always, since the birth of their first child, hovered over her like a swarm of angry bees. "It was not that I had really minded, of course, at the time. I'm old-fashioned enough to believe that a woman's place *is* in the home, not in the office. It's just that one gets so run down, spiritually as well, without even noticing it—without having *time* to notice it I should say." Now, for the first time in many years, she could read a magazine through from cover to cover if she felt like it, at one sitting; she could have friends in for dinner without being conscious, as the evening wore on, of the great stack of unwashed dishes which would have to be dealt with when the final goodbyes had been said. Now, while the guests sipped their coffee on the verandah she could hear, as one hears a delightful, far-off tune, the sound of Joseph washing up in the kitchen. And every evening before the children were bathed and put to bed (always clean pyjamas, always a fresh and spotless towel), she sat down with them and read a story: one that they chose, however long, and not one that she had chosen because it was short and quickly gotten through. This hour with the children became very precious to her, and she would even linger over it, as one lingers over a delicious meal, asking the children questions about the characters, reading favourite bits again. The children responded gaily, affectionately, giggling with delight as she changed her voice and became the wicked old witch, the dwarfs, the three bears. She felt like a flower that had been tightly curled and suddenly, in the embrace of the sun, begins to expand.

Then too, there were the coffee mornings when she met the other faculty wives and discussed the advantages and disadvantages of life in the tropics; how difficult it was to get butter and tea, how easy to get fresh fruit. And, of course, they discussed the stewards. It took several weeks before she realized just how lucky they had been. Tales of broken crockery, sullenness, petty thievery; gradually it dawned on her that Joseph was something of a miracle, a paragon. Each week some new disaster was reported. One steward had been caught wearing his master's vests, another had burned a large hole in an heirloom tablecloth. Yet another had disappeared for five days and returned with no explanation at all (and was duly sacked). One woman, who had arrived only three months before, was on her eleventh boy, and *he* didn't seem at all satisfactory. She would come away from these coffee mornings feeling like a healthy woman who has just been regaled with stories of ghastly operations; she found it all hard to believe. But there was, of course, the initial experience, that first night, and almost as though she felt it necessary to defend herself, to justify her good fortune, she would recall her own lurid introduction and speculate with her friends on what would have hap-

40

pened if—? For she could, in truth, find no fault with Joseph at all. "As a matter of fact," she confided shyly to her
new friends, "he is far better at managing a household than
I am." Then she would smile her delightful smile and throw
up her hands in a pretty gesture of mock despair. It was as
though they had all been panning for gold and she, the
lucky one, had by chance discovered the richest hoard, the
deepest vein, was carrying Joseph's virtues around in her
pocket like a sack of golden pebbles. Every Tuesday, early,
before the sun had begun to beat down in earnest, she and
Joseph would set off in the station wagon for town. Wandering from shop to shop, a gay straw basket on her arm,
she did the weekly marketing. (And always Joseph behind
her like a cool black shadow.) She enjoyed these Tuesday
mornings, enjoyed the colourful pageantry of the busy
town, the gay clothes of the men and women—"black
Romans in bright togas. How pale and insipid they make
the Europeans look." She enjoyed bargaining with the boys
who came rushing up with grapefruit, limes, oranges; enjoyed haggling with the "Mammys" over vegetables. Sometimes they would go to the large open-air market where it
was her turn to wait quietly while Joseph quickly bargained
for yams and sweet potatoes, bananas and pineapples. (He
had explained to her, very politely, that the prices were
raised for a white woman, and he could therefore obtain
more value for her money if he bargained for her; said all
this in a manner which indicated full recognition of this
deplorable practice and yet somehow managed to convey
the idea that such bargaining would be a pleasure for him
because it would serve her and "the Master.") Although
she could not understand what he said to the various traders,
she accepted his prices as absolute and would never dream
of interfering in these sometimes long and rather tedious
harangues. And if she needed something at the end of the

week, she did not hesitate to send him off alone, knowing that her money would be well spent and that he would not add on a sixpence here or a shilling there, as was the practice of many of her friends' boys. "There is something almost regal about him," she commented once to her husband. "It is as though everything that he does for me, for us, is done because he genuinely likes us, because he accepts us as people and not as employers. He serves without being servile—if you know what I mean."

They became familiar figures in the town, the small, fair woman in the straw hat and the huge black man. Even when she refused a purchase she would flash her smile and the sting was taken out of the refusal. And when the chattering, the crowding around became too much, she had only to turn to Joseph with a smiling, half-despairing look; a few sharp words in the vernacular and the vegetable boys, the fruit boys, the little crowd of beggars and loungers, would scatter like so many dark birds. It was wonderful to feel so protected, so well-looked-after. And of course, as though to keep her ever mindful of just exactly how wonderful it all was, there were always the Sundays—Joseph's day off. On Sunday morning there was no welcoming cup of tea, no immaculately laid breakfast table, no strong brown arms to deal with the tidying and washing up. On Sundays the magic world, her enchanted island as it were, disappeared. Joseph, like a huge black Prospero, retired to his cell, and she was left to work her own miracles. Strangely enough, in spite of the fact that she was rested and content, things always went wrong for her on Sundays. As though she were a bride of a few months, she found herself burning toast, over-cooking eggs, dropping a precious jar of marmalade on the floor. Jason and the children were really quite brutal about it, teased her unmercifully. "Who's Joseph's stand-in?" her husband would say to the eldest child. "I think she might

42

do for a small-boy, don't you, but she'll never make a cook-steward." At first she entered into the game, dropping serviettes on purpose, laying the table backwards, making faces and muttering, "Yes, Master, yes, Master," under her breath, or "Sorry, Master." But after a while it began to hurt a bit, this patronizing attitude of theirs, and one Sunday, when the youngest had wept bitter tears because Joseph wasn't there to chop up the eggs in a special way, she left the table in anger and wept a few bitter tears of her own. After all, in the terrible heat, with a cantankerous stove, they could hardly expect her to be perfect. However, they all filed shyly up to apologize and she soon forgave them with her brilliant, if this time somewhat watery, smile. Nevertheless, although she may have forgotten and forgiven, something remained at the back of her consciousness, something unnamed, unobserved, as infinitesimal as a grain of sand in an oyster, as quiet as the hum of a solitary mosquito. Monday came, Joseph returned to work and everything seemed, on the surface, to be back to normal. If a bit of the old magic was gone, she would have been the last person to admit it, perhaps the last person to understand why. And except for the incident of the snake, things might have gone on, indefinitely, very much as before.

However, one morning, as she made her way across the courtyard with a small basket of wet clothes (for she refused to allow Joseph to wash out her underthings, felt, somehow, that this was too much to ask any man to do), a large python sluggishly uncurled itself from the clothes pole not three feet away from her. For the space of a heartbeat she stood rooted to the spot, hypnotized with terror. Then she ran, screaming into the house. She was still locked in the farthest bedroom when her husband and the children came home for lunch. When she had been assured that the snake had been killed, she ventured forth and allowed herself to be

43

led to the table. The children were very excited, for apparently Joseph had killed the snake and it was stretched out on a pole behind his quarters. Already a group of admiring neighbours had been to see it and marvelled over its length and ugliness. It appeared that the eldest child knew all about snakes. "A python won't bite you, Mother. It crushes you to death. Or anyway, it crushes animals and things." He gazed at her with a condescending smile. But the terror of the morning was still so great in her mind that she scarcely heard the child, and his words bounced off her consciousness without wounding. She ate and drank mechanically and then, at her husband's insistence, went back upstairs to lie down. She had not yet spoken to Joseph, had not yet thanked him for killing the snake. To tell the truth, she was somewhat embarrassed about the whole thing. It was not that anyone would blame her for running away, for screaming, or even for hysterically locking herself in the bedroom. She knew that most people, men as well as women, have a violent reaction to snakes whatever their size. No, she was all right there, and her hasty retreat could hardly be called a social blunder. (As a matter of fact, the one woman on the compound who did show an interest in reptiles was thought by many of the others to be a bit "queer" and certainly slightly unfeminine.) Her embarrassment had to do with Joseph. Lying on the immaculate bed, shutters drawn against the glare, she faced up to the unpleasant fact that she did not want to thank her steward, that in fact she wished the snake had managed to get away. Now she was somehow in his debt, owed something to this dark man who could cope with anything. ("Something?" whispered a voice in her ear. "Everything.") She felt, for the first time, that she belonged to Joseph and not Joseph to her. And yet, the more she thought about it, the more she realized that the incident of the snake was just one example of the way in which Joseph had gradually made himself indispensable. Suddenly she heard the voices of her husband and the children, directly below the window. They must be coming back from viewing the snake, and the littlest child was obviously a bit frightened. "Will Joseph kill all the snakes, Daddy?" she heard him ask in an anxious voice. "Of course. That's what he keeps the big stick for." "But what will we do on Sundays?" said the child, and began to cry. "I'll tell you what," said his father, trying to jolly the child and unaware, of course, that he was being overheard. "On Sundays, if we see any snakes we'll take some of Mummy's toast and hit them right between the eyes. I should think they wouldn't come round here a second time." The child began to giggle, and all three moved around the corner and out of earshot. This was the crowning blow. Not only had Joseph made himself a necessity in their household, but he was making her a family joke. Each time that he increased in importance, she diminished. It was unbearable. She felt stifled, afraid. All the little helps which Joseph had performed for her, all the larger duties which he had removed from her weary shoulders—each act now seemed like a golden thread binding her tighter and tighter to a conception of herself as a totally incompetent, albeit delightful, woman. She felt as though she had been tricked out of her rights, deceived. She lit a cigarette and lay smoking, while she examined the problem, explored the wound the way a child will explore with his tongue the raw hole where a tooth should be. By tea time she had come to a decision.

The next morning, after her husband had left, after the children had been kissed and put on the bus, she gave Joseph a pound note and asked him to go into the market for some fruits and vegetables. She stood at the window for a long time, watching his erect figure grow smaller and smaller until he turned the bend in the road and disappeared.

Almost regretfully she opened the silver chest and selected three coffee spoons, holding the heavy silver in her hands for a moment, hating to part with it for even a few hours. Then, with the spoons in her pocket, she made her way slowly, determinedly, across the courtyard toward the servants' quarters at the back of the house.

OMO

I don't know, I just don't know. But maybe it isn't such a good idea—letting Negroes in the P.C. At least without warning them it won't work—they can be as outstanding as hell back home but what happens when they don't stand out at all—not physically—and are so tuned in to the idea they're different they can't change even if they want to? And Walter did. Walter really wanted to change. In this whole mess that's the one thing I hold onto—am absolutely certain of. If he didn't know what he wanted to change—or whom—if he just struck out blindly like a little kid hitting the chair he's just tripped over—how does that make him different from the rest of us? Yet, for him, it will be different. Another two or three days, when the newspapers get the story, back home (God knows what they'll do with it here), the differentness of Walter will sell extras or at least late editions. If it had happened to me, it would be news—happening to him it becomes sensation. And what will I say when they reach me?—it won't be long. "Tell me, Mr. Jonsson, did this boy seem disturbed to you in any way? Was he depressed, did he show signs of being unbalanced?" Can I call on the Fifth Amendment? Can I refuse to answer on the grounds that my answer would be so complete it would run into column after column and give them something they will only smell the surface of? I will refuse to answer. Just monosyllables. For if I hadn't found the diary,

47

and read it, I probably wouldn't have had the kind of answer I now hold—not even thinking back, and deeply. Or I could run. Or I would if I could. Not toward the city—but out toward the bush and Walter. Surely the bush is big enough here to hide more than one escaping slave? I know one thing. If I stay here any longer drinking this cheap gin and reading, re-reading, devouring his diary, I'll be in the correct maudlin state when they arrive, in rented cars with their tires screeching to a halt (I wonder if they'll miss the house because of all the corn growing). UP AP. BAM, BAM, BAM. "Open up Mr. Jonsson. We know you're in there." As though I were the fugitive. And maybe they'll bring along my mother—or Dad. "Open up, son, we just want to talk to you." Nice people—Mother in an exclusive drip-dry floral print and Dad sweating (I sweat a hell of a lot too—hereditary I guess), fanning himself with his hat, determined to look on the bright side. If I shouted at them through the mosquito netting—"Go away. No bright side now for your bright little boy. No right side either. All wrong, wrong, wrong. Nothing but wrong and stupidity and your dear son too busy with his own goddamn affairs to reach out his hand to his brother. Yeah—you heard me—his brother. Wasn't that what you taught me—isn't that what this farce is supposed to be all about? Walter—my brother, I—Walter's. Bullshit." Have another drink, Mr. Jonsson. Thank you, Mr. Jonsson, I will.

Once, when I was young, light-years ago, and sick in bed with mumps, my mother gave me old copies of some women's magazine. I cut them up, pasted food pictures, pictures of cars, animals, on sheets of white card—you know the sort of thing. Anyway, at the back there was one little bit for children, a picture of a naughty boy or girl doing something anti-social like teasing the family cat or splashing mud on a clean floor. There was a caption above and below, and two little birds, self-satisfied looking things, on either side. The caption read (above): THIS IS A WATCH-BIRD WATCHING A MUD SPLASHER; (below): THIS IS A WATCHBIRD WATCHING YOU. WERE YOU A MUD SPLASHER THIS MONTH????? Those birds really used to frighten me—fat, beady-eyed, approved by my mother's favourite magazine. I even dreamt about them sometimes. And now I sit alone—except for Walter's diary—and stare at the wall. Whereon is written, in Walter's writing (but only I can see it)—THIS IS A WATCHBIRD WATCHING YOU. The more I drink, the clearer it becomes. Six, seven years old, waking up in the dead of night, Walter watching me, E.K. Jonsson, mud splasher, cat teaser, convicted of a hundred crimes against humanity. Why couldn't it have happened to someone else?

Walter in his diary: "To be a slave in the physical sense may be exhausting and degrading, but it is vastly preferable to that other condition—being a slave to oneself. In the first case one can retain one's spiritual liberty, the only kind, after all, that counts." No, Walter, my buddy, my friend. A slave is a slave is a slave. And whatever kind of slave you want to make him, he has to sleep sometime. And when he sleeps, he dreams of his masters. That's why I mustn't drink too much—must stay awake. Watchbirds. Something you thought you had a monopoly on. If I go to sleep I'll see you, Walter—head, bird—Shape. I wish you'd go away or tell me what to do.

Have—another drink? Thank you, I will.

I first met Walter Jordan at Berkeley, when we were all training to come out here. Naturally we speculated about him—who wouldn't, under the circumstances? He was the only Yale man in our group and nobody could find out much about him. The girls thought he was handsome—he wasn't really—not in the face. I'd say he was too negroid if it wouldn't sound ridiculous. But you know what I mean. Lips too thick, brow too heavy. Not a Sidney Poitier at any rate. But he had a terrific build—tall, lean, could walk as if he didn't have bones but something else, supple and sponge-like, in his legs. And a terrific dancer. I've never met a Negro who wasn't a terrific dancer, but I don't think it's any "race heritage" thing. I'm sure there are plenty of Negroes who dance as badly as I do and who do as I do— stay off the dance floor whenever possible. Anyway, Walter never said much at bull sessions, or in the classroom, and so naturally we were all curious about him. Some thought he might be selected out because he was so quiet, but most felt he'd been sent on with the rest of us because he was a Negro and had volunteered and all that. It would've looked pretty bad sending him back. Sort of "stay out of our fight" kind of thing. So he went. Nobody (officially) ever said "Be nice to Walter" or anything like that; but we all went out of our way to do just that, wondering to ourselves just what made him join and whether we could live up to him. Yeah. That was another crazy thing—we all had this idea that he would succeed where we might fail. And the girls—of course— they went out of their way to be nice to Walter because he was so remote and romantic, and such a terrific man on the floor. Still, maybe their motives were more sincere than some of ours. I, personally, never had much to do with him back there, not because of colour but because he went to Yale. My father went to Yale, and my grandfather; but Yale put me on the waiting list and meanwhile I got a scholar-ship to a place in the Midwest and accepted it. Professional jealousy, you might say. Still, on the plane out he livened up a bit, brought out a guitar (which was not unusual, half the group carried guitars I should think) and played some great classical stuff (which was unusual, most of the others being of the "thrum-thrum" and a strong clear folk-song variety).

Then when we got here we discovered, Walter and I, that we had been assigned to the same school about 200 miles up from the capital. The group split up and headed off in various vehicles for their appointments, and Walter and I set off by plane for this place. The headmaster met us and explained that as accommodation was scarce we would share the same house outside the town. As far as I can recall Walter hadn't really said anything since we touched down at the international airport (what was I expecting him to do—kiss the ground? Burst suddenly into the vernacular? Cry "Mother!"?), but I remember he looked at the headmaster and then at me and then nodded, without smiling. I thought "Oh, God, he's embarrassed," and chattered away in the taxi like a damn monkey, trying to put him at his ease. He just looked out the window—great storm clouds were building up for the first of our many downpours—and smiled absent-mindedly in my direction now and then. This is what he wrote in his diary that night:

"So it seems I am to (literally) share my lot with E.K. He is not a fool, so why does he act like one? To put me at my ease? If so, he underestimates my patience. I think he is thrilled by the idea of actually living in Africa with an 'Afro-American' or whatever term people like E.K. use when they think, to themselves, about people like me. Does he expect my reactions will be different from his? Thus far I should imagine they are roughly the same: a sense of heat, and wet and greenness, of a slightly rotten smell in the air, of ears still tender from that Dakota. Still, I must not prejudge him. He wants very much to be friendly—as though he were the host and I were the guest. Asked me, with a smile (and he has a nice one—very straight teeth and very white), which rooms I preferred. He even said, 'preferred.' Then we had a beer (no filter here as yet, and the manual says filter and then boil) and went our separate ways."

This kind of minority pompousness was, I admit, never evident to me. Still, Walter writing was not Walter talking. I wrote a letter (he probably did too) and then was so tired I turned the light out and lay in the dark trying to unwind. The rain had stopped and the insects were just tuning up. Also the frogs. I could have been back at summer camp except that it was about ten times hotter and twenty times noisier. But the difference was one of degree really. I even had that first-night scared-elated feeling I used to get as a kid. Then I remember thinking, "Christ, you're really here. This is Africa," and fell asleep.

"This is Africa." You know, you try to look back on first impressions and of course it's impossible—you know too much later on—or you know a lot more, yet not enough. What I mean is, I'm not sure what I meant by "this is Africa." The house was really terrible-looking, pale pink stucco on the outside and every conceivable pastel on the walls inside—even a mauve in the bathroom. But we had a fan, and a refrigerator, and a real toilet and bath, all of which we inspected that first night. So "this is Africa" shouldn't have conjured up a vision of mud huts and natives. I guess the insects and the heat and the rain fitted in, though. I used to be a real Stewart Granger–Humphrey Bogart fan and expected these. Anyway the next few weeks are just a haze of colour and light and heat—and of course the rain. Our school was eight miles from the house, and we had to pay a taxi a really fantastic fare to take us back and forth. Another Peace Corps myth exploded. "Our boys and girls won't have cars or motorbikes, except in very remote areas. They will rub shoulders with the natives and enrich their experience."

Walter writes, after we'd been there several weeks: "Those executives in Washington who think that we will get to know the people by riding on their transport are very much mistaken. Know about them, maybe, but that's not the same thing. And the idea of rubbing shoulders with *anyone*, in this heat, is repugnant to us. The lifts we get are mostly from Europeans, while the moneyed African passes us by going so fast, usually, that I doubt very much if he sees us as more than just another blur on the side of the road. Often we walk as far as we can and then take a taxi—for an exorbitant fee. Even E.K., who is very enthusiastic about meeting the real Africa (though he has yet to define this term satisfactorily to me), agrees. Yet once a week he dutifully climbs aboard a Mammy wagon—much the same way as once a week he writes his letter home—out of a desire to gather and immortalize local colour. Sometimes I go with him (sometimes not) and we jolt slowly, painfully, thigh against thigh, into town. Immediately we get to school E.K. retires to a corner of the staff room and jots down his impressions in a little notebook which, like his camera, he carries with him wherever he goes."

Moral of the story: never room with a guy who keeps a diary. But if you don't know? I never saw the thing until three days ago. He wrote it at night, I guess, in bed. He never mentioned it to me or Miranda or anyone else. Yet he thought I was funny, carrying my notebook around, and I, like the fool I am, read him bits aloud, toward some of which he was very complimentary. When I first read the diary I was in such a state of shock it really didn't bother me —all the patronizing comments about E.K. doing this and that. Then I got bitter, and now I'm just surprised. Still, if I taught English like Walter, instead of math, I'd red-pencil the whole thing. It's so damn pompous and patronizing. I mean, I can't say he was a hypocrite—he never said he admired me or anything. But he never said he didn't. That's a kind of hypocrisy, isn't it? To live with a guy for over a year and write down blasts against him when he's asleep across the hall? I'd rather he talked about me to someone instead of having this private joke with himself. If he came back now I'd knock him down—just once—to let him know I've read it. If he came back. No. Mustn't think like that. It's better this way.

We had breakfast together, Walter and I, and rode to school together (usually) and came home together (at first) and ate together. We complained to one another about the staff toilets, or lack of them, and how it wasn't right we had to use the cinema john across the road from the school. We talked a lot, really, when I think back on it—but mostly about safe stuff—externals—like the heat and the price of beer and how much we could spend to paint the inside of the house. He showed me a picture of his family once, early on. Nice-looking mother and a real knock-out of a sister. His father had the same ugly-handsome face as Walter, but not the terrific body. He came from upstate New York some place and his father was a teacher. I asked him what made him decide to go to Yale and he said "scholarships" and dropped it. He had a way of dropping things he didn't want to talk about. He just turned himself off, if you know what I mean, and it was useless to continue. Once, I remember, two other volunteers stopped in on their way from the north (we always had visitors because we had a house, and that meant a free bed). One of this particular pair was a Southern girl, Ruth-Ann, whom I hadn't warmed to at Berkeley and didn't like much better when I saw her alone. Bright though —but nosy and a real thing about being Southern and in Africa. Her duty, etc., etc. Anyway, she was washing up in the kitchen and suddenly came out, hands all soapy, to look at us three in the sitting-room. (The other fellow was a Jewish kid from the Bronx. Very young and brilliant—a damn nice guy and a hell of a poker player.) Ruth-Ann stands there in the doorway and laughs her soft Southern-belle-type laugh. "I was thinkin' of why I came and wonderin' if you-all had motives as selfish as mine. I know why Larry came, we've talked about it; but why'd you come, Walter? Was it for a white reason or a black one?" I looked at her, a kind of scared feeling beginning in my chest; but then at Walter—hadn't I always wanted to ask him that myself? He just did the turning-off bit, laughed and took down his guitar. I don't know if Ruth-Ann really expected an answer or just felt that Walter expected, or deserved, the question. Anyway, answer or no, she could still write home to Mama that she-all had a weekend with E.K. and Larry and Walter, the American Negro she'd told them about. I think that's all she wanted—to be able to write home that she'd spent the weekend at our place. Still, I was disappointed that Walter wouldn't open up and give us some reasons. Even in his diary he doesn't comment on why he came. But he was writing to himself and already knew. It would have been illogical to put it all down there if he was sincere about it and wrote only for himself. Miranda knows. Miranda knows a lot of things and I must see Miranda soon and tell her what has happened if she hasn't already figured it out for herself. Maybe she knows and that's why she is staying away—in case he's here—and hiding. I'll have to get in touch with her tomorrow.

He has one entry which shows he was delighted with "old Africa" or whatever name he'd call it, so maybe he came, like me, just to look and see.

"Today," he writes, "I leaned against a wall for two hours and watched the women crossing to the old market. Barefoot, unselfconscious, immense loads of yams, tomatoes, tinned milk, you name it, on their heads. Often a baby slung behind sleeping, like some small opossum clinging to its mother's tail—content just to be. And often a small child walking beside, it too loaded down with the day's goods, yet it too with that intensely royal posture these women have. Miranda, if she had been with me, could, but probably wouldn't, have pointed out the signs of malnutrition, of early aging and incipient TB. But to me it was all gaiety and colour and purpose. I could have stayed all day, but the heat and the noise and the smells made me drowsy and thirsty. After I stopped for a drink I caught a lift home, where E.K. was, as I had promised myself, stripped to his waist, sweating profusely, already on his third bottle of beer and half-way through his weekly letter home. He types it single-spaced, on an air-letter, and often reads aloud bits which he has incorporated from his notebook. E.K. sees Africa as a picturesque ruin, not a living entity, something which you 'do' and then write up for the folks back home. Yet who is to say he is wrong?"

I can't tell here if he agrees or disagrees with what he thought was my point of view. Not that he understood it anyway. Of course I think it's "picturesque" here—you'd have to be blind or blasé not to think so. But a ruin? I don't know where he got that idea. Anyway, if it's being ruined, it's being ruined by the Africans themselves. But that's another story.

That's his first reference to Miranda, which is funny, because he mentions how we met her later on. I don't know when he went to the market, but the casual way he says Miranda would have shown him things sounds as though it was after we'd known her some time. Why didn't he put that entry first—the one where he describes our meeting? He must have left blank pages and then gone back and filled them up. Which is a funny thing to do. But Walter is or was —Christ which tense do I use?—a funny guy.

We met her in the third month, I remember that. And I remember the day. I was making one of my "dutiful journeys," as Walter calls them, and this time he was with me.

The Mammy lorry was loaded to the brim—crazy things they are—sort of crates on wheels and if you're travelling behind one you can see the women's bottoms bulging out the back. Chickens, yams, kids, anything, they pile it all in. We squeezed on somehow, but the damn thing (or so we thought at the time, not knowing we were going to meet Miranda) broke down just past the first roundabout. Nobody really cares when something like this happens— they've got an incredible talent for just waiting around— but I was cursing and swearing because we were supposed to get to school on time—set a good example and all that— and now we'd have to find a taxi. Off it all came—humanity and produce—and everybody arranged themselves and their belongings by the side of the road. I was looking up and down, trying to see a taxi, when one screeched to a halt (I don't think the average African realizes what brakes are for) and nearly knocked me down. I was about to try a few curse words in the vernacular when this pretty girl leaned out and asked if I wanted a lift. I thought she meant both of us—"do you want a lift"—but she looked a little surprised when I signalled toward the crowd.

"Not all of you," she said, and smiled. She had a really terrific smile. Then I realized—and I think it was the first time I really took it in—that Walter, at a casual glance, could be mistaken for an African. "No," I said, feeling stupid but determined, "just my room-mate, Walter," and she looked relieved. Probably thought I was some kind of "I won't ride while others walk" religious nut, which is not my policy at all. I'm too much of a materialist to go in for the missionary bit. And anyway, you should see some of the missionaries—the far-out Californian sects for example— whooping along in their Cadillacs, etc. She said she had to go to the hospital and would we mind a detour, Walter asked if she were ill and she said no, she was a nurse, flashing that fabulous smile again. You could almost see Walter thaw and I was feeling pretty terrific myself and trying to remember the name on that particular Mammy lorry so I could take it whenever I had the chance. I think it was "God Sees All" or something like that. They all have slogans painted on the back and some of them are really great—like "Next Time" or "Psalm 147" or "Too Late." Nobody seems to know why they do it. Anyway—we went up toward the hospital and let her off, but not before we'd found out her name and asked her to lunch on Sunday, whereupon, says Walter, "E.K. gave her so many directions as to how to find the house I'm convinced she will get discouraged—or lost." This is a later entry, where he says we'd met a "very pretty girl with a beautiful name." Actually, he's pretty amusing about my efforts to impress her. I was really keyed up and considering the fact I'd only just met her I guess I must've seemed a bit of a nut case. Particularly as I'm not usually a girl-chaser and kind of shy, really. Here's what he says:

"Since Thursday E.K. has been cleaning the house, trying on colourful shirts (finally deciding on white because she's English), and peering at a copy of *Escoffier* which he managed to borrow. He finally decided on *coq au vin*—this decision necessitating a hurried trip to the market for the essential *coq*, which he brought back, live, in a taxi. Very triumphant until he remembered that somebody was going to have to kill it. At first I refused, but after suffering his mournful face for half an hour (the bird meanwhile running wild in the kitchen) I suggested we *both* kill it and dress it, which we did, not very efficiently, E.K. holding and I cutting off the head. Neither of us could eat any supper and even now, after half a bottle of whisky, I can feel the warm blood pouring over my hands. The kitchen is thick with white feathers, but we've decided to leave it until the morning."

God, I remember that part. I'd never killed anything before, and neither had he, I think. I really felt terrible; but it
was worth it, because Miranda thought the dinner was great
—or said so anyway. I don't know what it was supposed to
taste like but it seemed all right to me. Anyway I was too
keyed up just having her here to care much about food.
Walter doesn't write anything about that evening, but he
had a good time too, I know it, and didn't turn himself off
once. She stayed quite late and we sat around, with candles,
drinking beer and listening to Walter play his guitar. God,
she was easy to be with, right from the beginning. At peace,
kind of not all keyed up and tense and trying to impress—
like so many American girls. I tried to imagine her as a
nurse (actually she's here training native nurses) but couldn't
picture her being at all brash and efficient. She came out
with some palm wine the next week and invited us to a party
the nurses were giving. Both of us, though Walter tried to
get out of it and said he was too busy. Anyway, we both
went and had a good time—at least I did, and I think Walter did too, though he was obviously falling for her himself.
I didn't keep it any secret from him—at first—how I felt
about her. He writes: "I watch E.K. and Miranda dancing,
E.K. not a very good dancer. [I accept that, I'm not.] Arthur
Murray course or dancing school when he was young. [Both,
and a fat lot of good it did me too.] When it is my turn I can
feel E.K.'s eyes on my back, hating me as a moment ago I
hated him. [I don't accept that. I felt jealous maybe, that
she was dancing with him and that he was such a terrific
dancer.] I realize that I've never held her in my arms before
and suddenly I am all left feet and bandaged hands and cannot dance—really dance—at all. I take her back to E.K.,
and excuse myself on the grounds I have to go to the men's
room. There I met a curious man—like a ghost. Miranda
knows him and says his name is Omo. He's an albino."

59

Omo. I wish to God we'd never gone to that dance—or really that Omo had never gone. Miranda told us about him, but he gave me the creeps, right from the beginning. When Walter came back he said, "I've just seen a white man," and not knowing what he was talking about we looked at him as though he'd had too much to drink. There were other white men at the dance besides me—these African girls are really lovely, some of them, and terrific to dance with or watch doing the "highlife." It's a sexy dance anyway, and they wear these long, tight two-piece dresses—really colourful. "No," he said, "don't look at me like that. You and Miranda, you're pink. A really white man." And then of course Miranda laughed because she knew whom he was talking about. Omo. One of the anaesthetists. There are quite a few albinos about, now that I'm aware of them, but when Miranda pointed him out to me, I was quite shocked. It wasn't so much that he was white, with that fair, kinky hair. It was that he looked kind of poached, if you know what I mean. A sickly colour, and he was wearing dark glasses. He was short and sickly-looking, but he had quite European-looking features. Miranda also said he was a half-caste (but I don't see how this could be, myself) and nobody knew much about him.

After that we kept seeing him—almost as though he were following us—or haunting us. And I know he bothered Walter. He wrote several times—"We saw the albino today, the one they call Omo." "Today I was crossing the street just as Omo was coming from the opposite side." Again, "He always wears dark glasses. Miranda says the light must hurt his eyes." And once, scrawled across a page, just "Omo, Omo, Omo," and underneath—

"Alb
Albatross
Alcatraz

Albumen
Albigenses
Albert Jordan" [His father's name.]
You don't have to be literary to figure that out, and that the guy was really bugging him. If I became conscious of Walter being black when Miranda first offered me a lift in the taxi, I think maybe Walter first became conscious of it when he called Omo a white man at that dance. He began to beg off going out with Miranda and me. At the time I—stupid bloody fool—thought it was to give me a clear field. I had no real idea how he felt about her—I knew he liked her but couldn't imagine (ironic as it may seem, for I was aware of how special she was right from the beginning) anyone liking her or loving her as much as I did. One time he refused to go to her place for dinner and I got sore—I wanted to be alone with her, but thought her feelings would be hurt. I never considered his. We'd gone a lot of places together—the market, the zoo, the stool village, movies—before this, and he has recorded it all, with no real comment, in the journal.

"Miranda sends us a note, by a friend, to invite us to dinner Sunday night. I complain of too much marking and beg off. But E.K. says I will hurt her feelings and if I don't want to go I will have to write a reply, which he will deliver. When I finish my note, all very friendly and polite, it occurs to me that on the face of it—two pieces of white paper, hers and mine, covered with the little footprints we call words—there is nothing to show that in the one case the pen was held by small white fingers, and in the other, by my own—large, pink-palmed and black. E.K. came back late, making lots of noise to attract my attention, but I didn't feel like getting up and turning on the light."

Even if some place inside I knew that he was unhappy it never occurred to me to think in black-white terms. I mean,

61

I guess I did know he was jealous—but Miranda treated us, then, so much alike I guess I was flattered by the idea that it seemed to him she favoured me when I couldn't see it. Maybe it never struck home that he could really want Miranda the way I wanted her—for keeps. Oh, there are lots of Africans with European wives (but mostly British) out here, and some whites with native wives. But Walter, black, was out here among blacks and I guess I thought if he went for anybody he'd go for a native girl—they're really lovely, some of them. No, that's not true, I didn't think about it at all. I was too tied up with my own problems. Like he mentions one incident I don't even remember. I mean, I remember the day, but not what he says happened.

"Linda, one of the prettiest volunteers, stopped in today on her way up to the North. She's been on the coast for the weekend and is one of those lucky blondes who tan so beautifully. We were playing Monopoly and drinking beer when E.K. said, 'You look terrific in that white dress. It makes your tan look almost black.' Embarrassed silence while I calmly throw the dice and land on *Chance*. 'Go directly to Jail. Do not pass Go. Do not collect $200.' Still, E.K.'s innocent remark (what else could it have been?—he's not subtle) opens up new areas for speculation. Coney Island in the sun. Thousands of pinky-white Americans blasting themselves with Skol and baby oil, trying to reach the point where the E.K.s of this world will say to them, in all innocence, on Monday morning, 'God, you're positively black.' Me, Walter, running out of the sea and shouting, 'Look, it's easy, don't go to so much trouble, I'll trade you my skin for yours.' Who would listen, I wonder, and agree?"

I'd better have another drink. I shouldn't really re-read the stuff, it's so bitter. But I never knew, not until the end, what was really bugging him. And I swear I don't remember saying that. I remember Linda (who wouldn't?) but not

62

the dress and not the crude remark. Or the "embarrassed silence." Surely I could remember such a thing? Some time after this, there was a terrific storm over the city and—which was not unusual—all the lights went out. Walter and I were up late preparing lessons when a hell of a bang went and then a crash, then darkness. We stumbled around looking for candles—which we didn't find until the next morning—then gave up and, with the flashlight which we always keep by the front door, went out to see the damage. After the bang, the rain seemed to slacken off, but we were still soaked through by the time we got through our little corn field and reached the main road. A bloody great tree seemed to be lying right across the road, and we were just debating whether to try to set up flares when we heard a sound—kind of an animal noise—practically next to where we were standing. Walter flashed the light around fast and then we saw it—a motorbike, all twisted, and underneath it something that looked like a man. By pushing and pulling we managed to raise the tree a few inches and twist the man free. It was really horrible. Rain and sweat in our eyes, and each of us taking turns holding this puny little light while the other pushed. And the body was all soft and broken like a doll or a dead kitten. I ran off for help and asked a Lebanese down the road who sent his car and driver back with me. How long Walter stood there in the darkness, guarding a man he couldn't see, I don't know. It must have been worse for him than for me. At least I was doing something. Anyway, Walter picked up this fellow and carried him to the car—a really immaculate new Chrysler, and we were a mess. We went along in case the police wanted a statement, holding the man across our knees so he wouldn't get bumped too much. The hospital has its own generator, and the light, after all that darkness, made our eyes hurt. An intern put the man on a stretcher and we just stood there in

63

the hall, dripping wet and covered with red earth and twigs, waiting for somebody to question us. The driver waited outside in the car. The injured man made another whimpering sound, and then a sort of gargle. And died. Walter turned to me and said, "You have blood on your hands." I looked down and saw that I did. I suppose that he did too. But the blood and this guy on the stretcher and nobody else around suddenly got to me and I was sick all over the corridor. Then we heard a voice and there was the albino. I don't know. It all fitted somehow. Walter looking like a tramp with his torn shirt and dripping clothes and me with vomit all over myself. And the dead man on the stretcher. Then this Omo, this albino, coming. I remember thinking, relieved, it's all right now—just a nightmare, none of this is really happening. But of course it was. Miranda had told us he worked at the hospital so I shouldn't have been shocked, but I was. He didn't say much, just looked at Walter, then me, and then went over to the dead man. "Was he a friend of yours?" he asked, and his voice was as queer as his looks—rather high-pitched and effeminate, but with a Scottish burr almost. We told him what had happened—or I did—I remember now, Walter didn't say anything and I did all the talking. Omo told us to go home, took our address, and said the police would get in touch. So we walked away down the corridor, leaving the dead man and Omo, and the driver took us home. We didn't even try to take baths or anything. Just rooted around for the whisky and went to bed. I can't remember that we said more than two words then, and the next day, when we saw Miranda and told her (I mentioned Omo, I think), it sounded as though it had happened to someone else. The tree remained for over a week, with just a narrow piece, the width of a truck, sawn out of the middle. Then they came with a fork lift and took the rest away. I was glad, because I couldn't bear to look at it.

Walter doesn't say much in his diary: "Yesterday there was an accident. A man died and Omo and I came face to face once more." And then, "E.K. is a brave man, but why did he suggest going for help? Is he a kind one, and quick-witted as well? Coming out of the darkness I might have been attacked as a thief." I thought nothing, consciously. But maybe he's right, maybe I knew no-one could question my motives. No, it's not true. His poison infects me. I thought nothing. I didn't know how to think—then. Anyway, Miranda told us some village had finally claimed the body—we were worried at first and wondered if we should arrange to bury him if nobody answered the ad in the papers. And life goes on, you've got to give it credit for that.

On Walter's birthday Miranda gave him a beautiful African cloth—something he'd wanted but hadn't bought. They're pretty expensive. He didn't try it on (she came to dinner that night and it was just like old times—we were all, I think, very happy) but went into his room and hung it up on the wall facing his bed. I don't think she meant him to try it on and she seemed very touched by his gesture. It really was a lovely thing—woven in four-inch strips as they do it here—all green and gold and scarlet. I must admit I wondered where she got the money for it—it must have cost her a lot—and I was a little jealous at the magnificence of her gift as compared with mine (I gave him a record of the Swingle Singers). Still, it was a happy evening, though Walter doesn't say anything in his journal. There are several blank pages after the accident and then he writes about a dance we all went to at the City Hotel (this was about three weeks later).

"Tonight, to impress Miranda perhaps, I wore the cloth she gave me for my birthday. It has been hanging on my bedroom wall where I can open my eyes every morning and without moving my head breakfast on the warm colours, stalk imaginary tigers in the jungle of reds and greens and yellows. We did 'highlife' at the City Hotel—even E.K., after he'd had a few drinks and forgotten he was shy. E.K., moving his hips self-consciously but surely among the shaking shoulders and melon-like bottoms of the girls was something to see. Because he is white, an 'Obronie,' he never lacks for partners if he feels like dancing. But Miranda wouldn't dance. She said she was tired and was content to watch. E.K. didn't like this too much but accepted it. He looks at her with what can only be described as dog-like devotion. And would I not be her devoted dog? She is the most charming person I have ever met and should be happy with E.K. if he ever gets the courage to ask her.

"About midnight, carried away by the noise, the beer, the scent of Miranda beside me, E.K. and his efforts, I decided to demonstrate my own prowess. Moving on to the floor without a partner, I hunched my shoulders and danced to the music until I felt it inside me and knew I could lead it, was a part of it. People stopped dancing—I could feel them stop and circle me though I kept my eyes nearly shut. Then my cloth fell off, revealing me in T-shirt and khaki shorts. Great laughter and applause from the crowd. I was sick, furious, and stumbled outside with my cloth to begin walking home. I heard E.K. and Miranda behind me, calling, so I ran until I found a taxi. And I have thought E.K. childish and absurd."

We ran after him but couldn't catch him. I was worried —I knew he felt humiliated but Miranda said he'd be better off alone. So we went to her place and talked—not about Walter, just life-in-general kind of things—and then I went home. There were no lights on and I wondered if Walter had come back. So I tried his door which was open and there he was all huddled up in bed as though he had the fever. The cloth was back on the wall. I didn't know what to say so I just got a couple of beers and sat on the edge of the bed, drinking. (I never saw his journal—it must've been under his pillow or in the drawer.) Finally he said, very far away, "It's all right," or something like that, so I left him and crossed the dining-room and went to bed. A few days later I got really drunk, after a particularly horrible day at the school (it was gradually dawning on me that I was not cut out to be a teacher, not a math teacher anyway, and the students had been giving me a rough time), and told Walter I wanted to marry Miranda.

"In a drunken 'heart-to-heart,' E.K. reveals to me what I have known all along—he plans to marry Miranda and will ask her at Easter. We sat on the edge of my bed (whoever designed the couch in the sitting-room didn't do so for comfort) while he chatted away about 'the marriage of true minds,' how wonderful she was, and so on. He kept trying to make it sound reasonable, almost sexless—a good arrangement—while all the time he blushed and stammered like a young girl, the virgin I suspect he is. After he had gone back to his room I rolled myself in my cloth and lay on the floor. I woke late, wet with tears and semen." He made fun of me to himself. That's what really shakes me. I know now a lot of it was just a cover (I sometimes wonder if he didn't write his journal to convince himself he was ironic and detached about everything). But I don't know if I can ever forgive him for making fun of me. If he came back, would I knock him down, or would I be too glad to see him? I need another drink to tell the next part. Have another drink, Mr. Jonsson. Thank you, Mr. Jonsson—may I have two or three? Be my guest.

Christmas came and went. We were both thoroughly fed up with the school, for different reasons, and celebrated by getting tight most of the time and taking Miranda to the movies. The garbage we sat through! Epics of this and that, crazy Indian love films, B or C grade, old Westerns. Christmas Eve I decided I wasn't going to wait to ask Miranda to marry me, but would ask her as soon as the ring was ready. I was having a special design made by a goldsmith in town, with all the local symbols on it. But he took his time—nobody hurries here except the taxi drivers. Meanwhile, on Christmas Day I went to the market. Miranda was coming to dinner that night. But I met her, then Walter. . . . Let Walter tell it.

"Miranda walks through the crowded market, her new sandals obviously hurting her, for every now and then she pauses, stands bird-like on one leg and rubs her foot. Each time she stops the line of children following her (in the hope of getting a penny) stops too. This goes on along the line of stalls, and I watch, unseen. E.K. comes around the corner, puffing heavily—it is very hot—his camera in one hand and a fistful of money to bargain with in the other. She sees him, halts, and they walk on together, the children following behind. As they pass the stall where I am busy bargaining for a string of prayer beads, I turn my head away; but Miranda calls, 'Here's Walter as well,' and forces me to walk along with them. The thing begins to look like Farmer-in-the-Dell. Miranda is looking for some presents to send home—she has been too rushed to want to shop before. She buys a huge straw hat for her brother, a Northern smock for her sister, who is expecting a baby in March. She holds the smock against herself for size—blue with gold embroidery—and smiles. I try to imagine her in a blue smock, swollen with E.K.'s child, and turn away. We pause to examine a table filled with the giant snails which are considered such a delicacy here. Still alive, they move carefully over the damp leaves. Then the man Omo appears, from nowhere, and nods curtly to Miranda. She has told us he doesn't like Europeans, but now, filled with Christmas, she touches his arm and asks him to wait. We are introduced, and he gives a strange high-pitched giggle and says, 'Oh yes, the two young men from America. I didn't recognize you.' We can't see his eyes because of the thick glasses, but his mouth is thin and cruel. Miranda asks him what he's buying and he giggles (there is no other word for it) and says, 'Snails.' E.K. looks sick and we smile and move on. I felt his eyes following us, and why not? Even the children at school make remarks about our strange trio. Yet they are not wicked. This man gives off what can only be described as a scent of wickedness and decay. Or am I exaggerating?

"Dinner a success. E.K. is now an admirable cook."

Omo. Dinner was a success. Omo and snails. Even while I ate I kept thinking about Omo and the accident—and snails. I didn't think about Omo and Walter. Why should I? To me, then, there was no connection.

Last week the ring was finished. I dressed up for a surprise visit to Miranda. I showed the ring to Walter and he said it was beautiful and wished me luck. You know all these crazy things about walking on air, etc., that the crooners used to sing about back in the forties. Well, that's the way I felt, as though I were walking on air. At 7.30 (it was already dark) I set off for town. At 2.30, with the ring in my pocket, I returned. I was surprised to see a light on, but figured Walter was waiting up for me. I didn't really want to see anyone, just then, not even Walter, so I sneaked around to the back and let myself in the kitchen door. Then I heard voices and realized Walter had company. The other voice, without the face, I didn't recognize at first.

"It wasn't hard to find the way," it said, "since you were kind enough to give me your address. Or,"—it giggled—"your friend was kind enough." And Walter's voice, resigned, quiet.

"Why don't you get out?"

69

"But I came to see you, my friend. We are friends, aren't we? Almost brothers, you might say." Then the terrible giggle. I was too shocked to move. And curious, too. Yes, I was that all right. Curious.

"Almost," said Omo, "like brothers."

"I don't know what you mean."

"Oh come, come, come. You're not stupid. I know quite a bit about you, you see." Then, sharp and quick, "You'd like her, wouldn't you?"

"Don't you dare talk about—"

"Miranda? Why not? Isn't she your friend, and your friend's friend?"

"This has nothing to do with you. Please go."

"But I've come all this way just to see you! I saw him get out of the taxi and came right out to comfort you." Then, softly, "what do you suppose they're doing now, eh? Talking about mathematics? Or perhaps in bed? That's more like it, isn't it? In bed, maybe. No sheets on a hot night like this."

I found I had moved forward, then stopped at the sound of his voice, pitched even higher.

"No! You wouldn't hurt me. Sit down. I said, sit down— White Man!"

I couldn't move now. Walter's voice sounded very far away.

"I tell you, I don't know what you mean."

"And I tell you not to be so stupid, White Man."

I could feel him lean forward, almost hissing.

"Isn't that what you want to be, with your white friends and your long trousers and your fancy degree? Omo, like me. You know why they call me Omo, don't you."

"I know."

"Whiter than white. Your wash is whiter than white with Omo. It is not my name."

"It is not your name."

Walter, hypnotized in the sitting-room, I, hypnotized in the hall. The voice went on and on in little hiss-like sentences.

"Alastair's my name. Alastair Campbell. The man they call Omo. Would you like to know something about me? No? Too bad. Mine's an interesting story. My father was a missionary, a man of God. My father, man of God that he was, and with God on his side, made many converts—among them Comfort Mensah, who felt, perhaps simultaneously, the hand of the Almighty and the hand of my God-fearing father. But my father was an honourable man. He married the girl and had many brotherly-lovely children before he died of yellow fever. Many lovely children—all brown, and the pride of the mission. And one freak, Alastair, who killed his mother and broke his father's heart. When they took that white body out of that black, black womb, I think he considered it a judgment of God. He sent me away, back to his home in Scotland, paid for my education (where he got the money I'll never know). And when I wrote I wished to go into medicine he agreed without a murmur. All this done by letter; for never once did he—or anybody—come to see me. As a child at school I found I could only imagine him as a long tanned arm ending in a hand holding a fountain pen. A hand for signing cheques —not for writing letters. I wasn't popular at school. How could I have been? A freak with weak eyes, a boy who wore sunglasses, even in Britain, a boy who never received a brown paper parcel full of home-made cakes, or a few sweets. And in the end, a boy too weak to go on and study medicine."

"Why are you telling me all this?"

I had forgotten Walter, but now I, too, wondered why.

"Shut up and listen. So I trained as an anaesthetist and

came back here, to claim my 'inheritance' as it were, to be one of my mother's people—an African. I do my work well, speak the language now like the native I am, mingle with what your friend would probably call 'the people.' But I am set off by my skin, that white skin you covet so much, from a satisfactory relationship with anyone, black or white. The superstitious African views me as something special, a natural freak, and therefore endowed with supernatural powers. He shuns me as a friend, not because he feels I am lower than he is, but because I am higher, more powerful, closer to the gods—or devils." He laughed again, and each laugh hammered his words into my brain. Coffin nails. Why didn't I stop him? I don't know.

"The European cultivates me out of curiosity, tries to take my picture when he thinks I'm not looking. I frighten him. And I shun the European because for fifteen years the European with whom I should have had the closest ties existed for me as nothing more than a hasty signature. My father, the God-fearing man, the apostle of brotherly love."

"I'm truly sorry—"

"That you can't change places with me? Is that what you were going to say?"

"No."

"Well, it should have been. Don't be sorry for me, be sorry for yourself. Aren't you, eh—just a wee bit?"

"Will you have a drink?"

"It's about time." A giggle. "I wondered how long I'd have to wait."

My heart stopped. But whisky and glasses were in the sideboard and a decanter of water was on the table. They need not come out to the kitchen.

"That's better," said the voice. "Now you are showing some true brotherly love. Shall I tell you a story?"

"If you have to, and then I really must—"

"What?" Giggle. "Lie in bed and wait for your friend to come back? What will you think about, eh? He won't be back tonight. Forget it."

"Tell me your story." Walter's voice was deep and terrible and resigned—like the voice of somebody in terrible pain. I wanted to go to him and kick that little white fink down the front steps. But I couldn't. Anyway, I didn't.

"Have you ever killed?" he asked.

"No."

"I have, this afternoon. One of your kind—a white woman. A stupid bitch who shacked up with an African while her husband was on leave, and then discovered she was pregnant. Amusing, don't you think? The issue could hardly have been passed off as her husband's child, now could it?"

"But why?"

"You're too impatient, black boy. I'm coming to that. Why? Because she tried to get rid of it herself, and as is obvious from her original adventure—she was a bungler. They brought her in this afternoon for an emergency operation. I administered the anaesthetic."

"You mean you—"

"SHUT UP, BLACK BOY. I 'mean' nothing of the sort. I simply told her something as I leaned over and put the needle in. I whispered, 'Now you are going to be paid back for meddling with those who are not your own kind. I'm going to give you another present from a black man. I'm going to kill you, swiftly and efficiently, now, and in front of all these people.' She cried out, once, and then she died. It will be written off as a massive hemorrhage and heart failure due to shock."

The hairs rose on the back of my neck.

Walter said, "You frightened her to death."

"That's it. I frightened her to death." Giggle. "Aren't you shocked that someone as weak as I could do something as strong as kill?"

I heard Walter get to his feet.

"What's the matter, White Boy, don't you believe me? It's only begun for you. The hate and the bitterness that make you choke on your own bile. But it has begun. That's a step in the right direction, isn't it? Think about your friend, eh? And the girl. . . ."

"Get out." Walter was shouting. I heard the door slam. "Don't come back here, ever. You're mad. I'm not like you —I hate no-one."

"Love me then, black boy," said Omo, from outside the door. He began to cry. "All I want is some love, that's all." I heard Walter stumble, as though he were drunk, and then the heavy inner door slammed into place. Omo rapped on the door softly, then louder, but Walter had turned out the lights and gone into his room. I waited until the footsteps had died away, and then I inched down the hall and fell asleep with my clothes on.

When I awoke it was nearly noon and I thought Walter had gone on to school without me. The shock of Omo's appearance at our house, plus my own misery at being refused, however nicely, by Miranda, kept me drinking until late afternoon. When Walter didn't come home that evening I began to get worried. I looked in his room and all his books were on the table. His bed hadn't been slept in, but this journal was lying face-down on the floor. The last entry, the one with which I began, said "Must find Omo." Nothing more.

Three days ago they found him, his head bashed in from behind, in some bush behind a café. The proprietor, the papers said, could tell the police no more than that the man who was called Omo was sitting with a young African until they both got drunk. He thought they left together.

And Walter? He hasn't come back yet. I left food in the

refrigerator and the door open, and hired a car (I told the school I was sick with fever). With an interpreter I traced him to the north, driving day and night, and finally to a small village near the border. The village only remembers him as a strange young African, nearly naked, who squatted in front of their fire and tried to tell them something in a language they didn't understand. So I sit here and drink. Miranda may have been and gone—if she has seen the papers. She would know about it anyway; but how much did she know about Walter? How much did any of us? Anyway, I think I'll stay here now, for a while, and wait. For one thing the interpreter was sure of. The elders, when questioned, were certain that before he left he had told them one thing. He had told them he was going home.

THE ALBATROSS

We hid in our tiny bathtub and waited for the footsteps to move off down the path. Hugging each other from necessity, the curtain drawn as though we are simply waiting for the floodlights to go on—hero and heroine caught in the classic clandestine clinch. Rocking with silent laughter. Have you ever had to sneeze in church, been seized by insane giggling in the public library? It's very difficult.

"I know you are in there, my friends. Hello, my friends, are you at home?" A gargling-under-water way of pronouncing his words. "I told you it was Hermann," she hissed. "Shut up." How does he know? This is one window he can't peer into. Maybe he has rubber-soled stilts. No, keep quiet. He's only guessing.

Then the baby woke up, so we stepped gracefully over the rim and went to let him in.

"Well, Hermann, you're out late. Business pretty good, eh?"

"Business is not so good. I am thinking of getting out. Nobody buys these days." Nobody but bloody fools like us. Got your fat foot in the door that time, didn't you?

"Never mind, Hermann; have a cup of coffee. Margaret was just going to put the coffee on, weren't you, Margaret?"

Loosens his tie and eats up all the cakes. "You see my belly?" No, Hermann, we don't see it—sack of pudding with a head at the top. "I have lost some weight. Nearly ten

76

pounds. I have taken nothing but soups and salad all day."

"Have another jam tart, then, Hermann."

"Thank you, they are very nice. Margaret must make for my wife the receipt."

Dank you, dank you. You're a tank you Hermann. One of these days too many jam tarts will make for your wife de widow. How much insurance do *you* buy, old chap?

"Well, what brings you out at this hour, Hermann?"

"The Book. I was to myself wondering how the Book is coming on?"

"Well, Margaret's very busy with her term paper just now, aren't you, Margaret?" Vigorous nod. Hermann looks dejected. Margaret begins to wear her can't-put-a-dog-out look. Idea.

"Would you like to hear the last bit again? When the fuse blew we never got to replay it. Of course *we've* heard it several times since then, haven't we, Margaret?" Another vigorous nod. Funny how she lures them here and then clams up. Worth investigation. "You know, Hermann, you really need a dictaphone and secretary, doesn't he, Margaret?" Margaret weakening. My jellyfish wife.

"I don't mind, really, but the term paper and the baby keep me rather busy at the moment."

"It will make for us our fortunes. I know myself a man in Hollywood." Hermann knows a man everywhere, but his collar is frayed and he eats up other people's cakes.

I fiddle with the knobs and Hermann's voice, like Hermann's bulk, fills the little room. He beams and listens to himself. Solemnly. Over a second cup of coffee.

"I went to Greece by mistake. I was in the general hospital in Alexandria with an infection of the neck. My neck was full of pus. You know, you walk in the desert and the desert, it is very bad. And you sweat and the shirt begins to get stiff. Then you had the sandstorms, and the sweat and

77

the sand become one crust. Each movement that a man makes, it is like he is in a suit of armour. I think that most of us were infected, some more, some less. And they ask me when the pus is all gone, do I want to go back to my own unit? And they are very nice; they don't tell me that my unit is already in a poor spot. Because it was then the end of April and Greece collapsed two weeks after I arrived. I suppose it was on about the twentieth of April.

"In any case, the ship I am on went over there, and when I arrive everybody says, 'Why did you come? Everyone's retreating. Why did you come?' A mess.

"So—we retreated, and the retreat was no fun. We went down first by train, and every five minutes we were bombed —the planes coming down as low as they could. And it was like this all the way to Kalamata. And there the stories really start, for at once we were taken prisoner. And our own particular unit had the dishonour to be taken by Max Schmeling. Do you know Schmeling? He was a boxer who got knocked out by the late Max Baer. Well, Schmeling was a parachutist, I think a captain, maybe, and my unit was taken prisoner by this man. They bombed us for several days, and then we are ordered to go down to the jetty, where the Navy will pick us up and take us to Egypt. Around midnight we heard the ships—destroyers—coming in, and we are told to throw everything away, kit bags, guns (we were supposed to destroy our guns), gas masks—everything.

"And then they move out without us. I never find out why. They move out without me, and without my company, and that is that. There we were, still standing on the jetty. Our major and lieutenant disappeared, and after a while they come back, both crying like babies. They told us we should have faith in God and the King and some other things similar, and that our brigadier had surrendered. Naturally I, being of Austrian birth, was very unhappy about that. So I take my paybook—my identification—and destroy it. And I keep the gun. You might say that for legal purposes, such as being a prisoner of war in a German camp, Hermann ceased to exist."

Excited in spite of ourselves. Strange names, the exotica of war, Max Schmeling, bombs. Better than the late-late movie. Hooked again by Heroic Hermann. The tape runs out with a wistful pizzzz. "Come again, Hermann. Any time!"

"Thank you. Next time I will tell of how I move from the village to Larissa. Very exciting stuff. My friend in Hollywood will eat it up." Like cakes.

Mrs. Pilkinson, spreading her aura of expensive cheap perfume, never takes off her hat. Same hat always, three plastic cherries on black straw. You'd think she could be a little more adventurous, a plastic pumpkin perhaps for autumn, a small snowman at Christmas, a slice of plastic watermelon in summer.

"Excuse me for mentioning such a del-ee-kate subject, my dear, but does your husband use a deodorant?" Only after you've been here, lady. Five minutes with the Air Wick—after I check that the kid's still breathing. "Yoo-hoo, Avon Calling." Either my wife has a basic speech defect or she can somehow tune herself out.

"Why don't you say 'no' to these people once in a while?"

"Why should I?"

"They waste your time and that one wastes my money."

"They're interesting."

"Mrs. Pilkinson is *interesting*?"

"Yes, she is. And she's had a hard life. It can't be much fun going from door to door like that."

"Can't be much fun for all those husbands who have to come home to a house smelling like a 50-cent brothel."

79

"How do you know what a 50-cent brothel smells like?"

Touché. Never marry an intellectual. Or not one who's an aural nymphomaniac.

But then there's Hermann. Who could deny that Hermann is interesting? In Hermann my wife has found the jewel for her collection. Heroic Hermann, sucking the past like barley sugar. Hermann with a future like a cancelled stamp. Pilkinson can stuff herself for all I care, but Hermann has something. Sometimes.

". . . then I begin to get terribly sick from the malaria." We prick up our ears. Pavlovian reaction to Hermann has begun again. He should really be on "Zis Is Your Life." Wasted on us. And why should such diseases have these delightful names? Malaria, diarrhea, carcinoma, syphilis, beri-beri. Allow me to introduce my little daughter Diarrhea. Like characters in a Greek tragedy.

". . . a very high fever and couldn't walk. We had no quinine, no nothing. So they carry me into the church and the priest he puts all the holy icons around me and pours buckets of holy water over me. My three companions, they nearly die with laughing. I thought I too would die—but not from laughing. And then an old man comes with one of those straight razors—you know—that they use to shave with. So he, the priest, cut me in the centre of my forehead. A careful observer can still see the scar." Observe carefully. Hermann tips his round forehead upward to the light. The landlady's lampshade casts a rosy glow. We make ourselves believe that we can see it. My wife swears afterward that she can see it, so it must be there.

"First of all the blood came out—it looked as black as India ink and as thick"— tick, tick, tick, we watch the blood ooze out and hold our breath—"like syrup or molasses. He had put some kind of container under my head and asks me

80

hen to lean myself over so that this blood would drop into
t. And after maybe ten, fifteen seconds, when this black
blood had oozed out of the ugly wound, red blood came and
felt myself much better.

"Then the second thing he does is to knead my belly—
o give me a kind of massage of the abdomen. I did not have
a belly at that time, but let us say he kneaded the part where
my belly is today." Don't have to ask us to observe carefully
where your belly is today, do you? "It was very painful—
but in the end Hermann did not die of malaria."

'I really wish he did." Sleepy murmur from the heap of
blanket called Margaret.

"What—die of malaria? So do I sometimes."

Upright now, shocked and hurt. "Had a friend in Hollywood. You knew what I meant." Tomorrow I will buy myself one of those straight razors. You know ze kind?

"Won't you have some more potato salad?" asks the con-
sumptive young man who is building a cabin in the woods
and paints huge canvases on Mexican themes. They have
been to Mexico, and as we eat our delicatessen dinner, they
tell us about the colours, sights and smells.

"It is the smell of Mexico I really wish to capture."

Their twin girls eat with us, sitting on little wooden
home-made potty-chairs. Clever idea, I suppose, but I don't
think we'll stay for dinner next time. The wife wears Ber-
muda shorts and has a haunted look. She confides to Margaret that after she had the twins she spent two months
mentally incognito. Doesn't remember a thing. Wish I
could forget that plonk-plonk in the middle of a forkful of
potato salad. Must ask her how she did it.

At home we turn the television on without the sound. And

without turning on the lights. However, Hermann doesn't come.

Jesus keeps falling off the fuzzy-felt board, but the young man in black never pauses, just picks him up and rubs him gently back in place. They have declined tea and coffee. "I'm sorry, but it's against our rule." So we finish our coffee stealthily and I light a tentative cigarette.

"Oh, I come from New York State," says Margaret. I must have dozed off.

The two young men (are there really two or am I getting tired? Maybe they have to travel in packs, my brother's keeper kind of thing—make up for Cain) are very interested. Almost excited. One says, "Then you must have seen the place where he had his vision?"

"No," says Margaret regretfully, "I'm afraid not."

"It is my great dream," says the other (or is it the same one?), "to go to New York State and stand on the spot where he had his vision." Margaret argues theology with them. Discusses is maybe a better word. I watch her. Like the landlady's lampshade, she casts a rosy glow on all these people. Saint or nut—I wish I could make up my mind.

Jesus falls down again and is carefully picked up. I feel neglected.

"How long do you have to do this sort of thing?"

All three looked at me, startled, as if they had heard the voice of God walking in the garden.

"I don't, ha, ha, mean talking to Margaret and myself here. I mean travelling around to people's homes to explain your doctrines."

"Two years." They answer in unison. "And then we hope to go to Salt Lake City."

"After you go to upstate New York, of course."

Margaret glares at me. Not the voice of God after all.

The serpent. I hood my eyes and stare innocently back. They laugh modestly and show us the little book which explains the whole thing better than they can. "I really don't think —" Margaret gives them each a tube of Avon silicone hand cream as they leave. Bicycling all over like that and winter coming on. What the hell, we can spare it. What's a couple of tubes of $1.69 hand cream between friends. I put the book on the bottom row beside this month's *Watchtower*. Then I notice they've forgotten one of the disciples and have to go running down the road after them.

This sort of thing has got to stop.

"He searched us, and by some stupidity we had about three, four German pistols on us, so this gives them a very clear indication that we must have killed some Germans in order to get the pistols. So naturally he got mad." (Hermann, for Christ's sake, don't stop now, get on with it. The recorder whirrs softly as Hermann helps himself to another brownie.) "And took the machine gun from the armoured car. And as there was no wall he stood us against nothing in particular." (I do, too, Hermann. I wish you had a friend in Hollywood.) "And wanted to shoot us to kill us. And for why? Because we had German pistols. Well, he was ready for the execution, and we more or less figured that was the end of the story. I was thinking how stupid I was not to shoot somebody instead of giving myself up like that. To be caught and shot for nothing. To shoot back and be killed, at that time, is not so important. At least we would have defended ourselves and have wounded them. But to be shot like that? Like cattle?

"But before he was ready comes a small car with an officer. And the officer he started to argue with the NCO about the execution. And so, of course, in the end, we are ordered to get into the truck as he wants to find out where we get the pistols, from whom, etcetera. Once you are into the red tape procedure—the chances that you will then be shot are practically nil."

Hermann has done it again. We breathe a sigh of relief and Hermann beams like a harvest moon.

"You like it?"

"I don't think," says Margaret, mopping her forehead with the dress she is mending, "that 'like' is the right word."

"You think it will sell?"

Oh Hermann, Hermann the Austrian German, victim of the Great American Dream. But your story should have been written twenty years ago. You've sold us, Hermann. What is more important, you've sold me. Isn't that enough?

"How's business, Hermann?"

How in hell can he do any business when he sits around eating Margaret's brownies and drinking our coffee 80 per cent of the time? Hermann, my friend, to help you and to help ourselves I zink we'll have to do the bathtub bit again.

"Do you think we're using him?" says Margaret, drying the coffee cups.

"The question of who's using whom is an interesting one. And when are you going to finish that term paper if he keeps dropping in?"

"Any day now." She will, too, that's the trouble.

"Speaking of term papers, there's an English boy in my seminar..."

"*No.*"

"How do you know what I was going to say?" She examines a cup carefully.

"I do know what you are going to say. There's an English boy in your seminar and he has nowhere to go for Sunday

84

dinner. . ."

"Christmas dinner."

"Correction. Christmas dinner. And you thought it would be nice as there's only you and me and the baby and it's our first Christmas away from any of the family. . ."

"I'm so glad you see it that way. I was afraid you might object."

In the end he comes, with a big bag of apples and no pyjamas. I eat an apple, nude, sitting up in bed and listening to him snore away happily in the sitting-room. The aunts all send us thank-you letters for the Avon cologne and Margaret's sister writes from Boston that little Timothy hangs his turtle soap around his neck every night before he takes his bath. I wonder what little Timothy's going to think when that turtle's all melted away and he's left with a dirty great piece of rope.

We don't see Hermann over Christmas, but one night (must've changed to crepe-soled shoes, the bastard) he arrives with something that looks like a portable typewriter. Business, she must be looking up.

"I thought I would see what you think. The company has lent it to me." We settle down. Rather disappointing, I must say. No hair's-breadth escapes tonight. Hermann is up to somzing.

"You will sit here. And you, my dear Margaret, will sit yourself please here." Hermann adjusts the coffee table. The machine opens up and Hermann switches off the light.

"You see my friends, a record player-slide projector." The inside of the case is lined with some white stuff and Hermann settles himself between us. He throws a switch. A voice, not Hermann's, begins to speak.

"Here is a picture of John and Mary Doe and their two lovely children." (Gay Kodachrome of John and Mary smiling toothily at each other in tastefully furnished sitting-room. Children reading *Playboy* or something in the corner.)

"Ping."

Margaret jumps. "What's that curious 'ping,' Hermann?" Hermann has stopped the machine. We're right on cue.

"The 'ping' it tells me when to change the picture. Clever, no?" We resume.

"John and Mary and their two fine children live in a fine house on a fine street in Blankville." (Picture of fine house —exterior view—on fine Blankville street.)

"Ping."

"One morning John kisses his wife goodbye." (Kiss. Chaste close-up.)

"Ping."

"And sets off, as usual, for his office downtown." (Cut to John behind the wheel of his fine car.)

"Ping."

"Suddenly out of nowhere." (Car obviously out of control, not John's.)

"Ping."

"Comes a car." (Closer shot of nowhere car.)

"Ping."

"John swerves." (Picture of frantic John frantically turning the wheel.)

"Ping."

"But it is too late." (Nasty picture of two cars on top of one another.)

"Ping."

"Mary and the children are devastated."

"Ping."

"After the sad formalities of the funeral, Mary discovers that John has no insurance and her widow's pension is very small."

"Ping."

"The fine house in Blankville must be sold." (They goofed on this one; sign comes out as FOR SALE.)

"Ping."

"Mary must go to work."

"Ping."

"She moves from apartment to apartment with her two growing children." (Picture of sleazy apartment kitchenette with open milk carton on the table and the two kids with sad eyes eating peanut-butter sandwiches.)

"Ping."

"But it didn't have to be like this. Let us go back to that fatal morning when John kissed Mary goodbye for the last time." (Picture of John kissing Mary goodbye for the last time for the second time.)

"Ping."

"Yes, John crashed." (Same old crash.)

"Ping."

"And of course Mary was devastated."

"Ping."

"Ping."

"But after the sad formalities Mary found she had a friend." (Enter friend with a sad but toothy smile and bulging briefcase. I'm not sure Margaret should watch this sort of thing. Might give her ideas.)

"Ping."

"Her friend is the man from Transatlantic and he tells her that John has thoughtfully provided for her and the children." (Picture of Mary looking touched as she gazes at a cheque made out for $10,000.)

"Ping."

"The fine house in Blankville does not have to be sold." (Somebody took down that crazy sign.)

"Ping."

"Mary does not have to go to work." (Mary, slightly bored, reading a book.)

"Ping."

"The children do not have to be neglected." (Children smiling toothily over another issue of *Playboy*.)

"Ping."

"And all because John looked ahead and talked things over with the man from Transatlantic." (Picture of picture of John on mantelpiece of fine house. Children and Mary all gaze at him worshipfully. If John could look ahead, I wonder why didn't he take a taxi?)

"Ping."

"Mary's friend can be your friend too. Why don't *you* let the man from Transatlantic into *your* home?" (Picture of the man from Transatlantic smiling toothily at You and Me.)

Ping. Ping. Ping. Music.

"Do you think it will sell?" asks Hermann anxiously.

"It's certainly very novel." Trust old Margaret. I'd like to write a letter to the public about the man from Transatlantic. He'll help you to look ahead all right—sell you $10,000 worth of life insurance you can't afford and eat up all the bloody brownies in the house.

"Just great, Hermann." Margaret gets up. "Will you stay for coffee?" The man from Transatlantic loosens his tie and folds up his little machine.

Spring. The baby stands up for the first time, the landlady promises a new coat of paint, we plant a garden (much too early and nothing comes up but parsnips). The voice of the turtle is heard in the land, mingled with the voice of the tape-recorder as Hermann spends more and more of his time at our house, escapes from a moving train head first, lives with some shepherds on olives and cheese, is captured

88

again, escapes, tries to set sail for Crete and is captured again. I run out of tapes and have to buy some more, but the story goes on and on and on. And not just Hermann's story, but the story of the others—the old Greek woman who drops a precious egg into his hand and walks away before he can thank her in his faltering Greek—the famous brigand who had killed 23 men and lived as a proud and terrible outlaw in the hills. Our heads spin like the two reels on the tape recorder.

" 'And,' he said, 'when the war is over and you go back to your fatherland and your general says, "Where have you been all this time, during the war," what are you going to say?' So I said, 'It depends where I was.' So he says, 'You are going to tell him you are the whole war with me, that's what you're going to tell your general. And your general will say, "What man is this?" And do you know what you are going to tell him?' I said, 'Well, I would tell him, he was good man.' He said, 'Yes. You will say, "He was a *very* good man," that's what you are going to tell him. That's what you are going to say to your general.' So we were sitting there drinking. What could happen to us, after all? More than the killing of us, and we had been faced with that before! So he said then, 'After that, you will say to your general, "Don't you want to do something for this very good man?" And what will you tell him?' 'I will tell him yes.' And he said, 'Do you know what you have to do for me? You will tell your general to tell your king to tell the fucking bastard king we have here in Greece that all those mountains, where my sheep are, belong to *me* and to nobody else.' And I said, 'If my general asks me I will tell him.' But he never did."

This time it was little felt steps with names on them. The hierarchy of the church. Elders, deacons and what not, with

God at the top, of course. The little steps kept falling off. I was tired. It had been a bad day. The baby was teething and had eaten up some of Margaret's footnotes; we'd had a polite row about Mrs. Pilkinson's spring catalogue. ("If you think I'm going to support that bloody woman by ordering a dozen Castile Easter bunnies you're very much mistaken." That sort of thing.) I was also tired of watching those little steps fall down—and I wanted a beer.

"Say," I said to the earnest young man. "That fuzzy-felt board seems to be giving you a lot of trouble. Have you ever thought of trying something else, something really up-to-date and modern?" They looked at me politely. "Well, maybe modern isn't exactly the kind of word you'd take to."

"Oh no," replied one of the twins. "We pride ourselves on the fact that our church has something to say to a modern society." Dangerous word, pride. Pride goeth before an etcetera. I wonder, if you interrupted them in the middle of a sentence, would they have to start again?

"Well, I have a friend who has a dandy little machine. It's very light and could be easily carried in your bicycle basket. It looks like a typewriter, see, but when you open it up it's a portable phonograph and slide projector combined. While the record gives the spiel, slides flash on the screen— which isn't really a screen at all but the back of the box painted white. You could have pictures of Upper New York State, covered wagons, Salt Lake City, maybe the elders standing around on the steps. And it goes 'ping' when it's time to turn the slide. Could be a big seller." I gave them Hermann's card.

"I suppose you think you're funny," said Margaret's back, as the two bicycles disappeared down the road.

"Well, I think I'm funny-ha-ha and not funny-peculiar like some people I won't mention. But it could put a little life into their routine, couldn't it?"

"Once upon a time there was a Man." Picture of earnest man gazing at fertile farmland in Upper New York State.

"Ping."

"This man had a vision." Out-of-focus sunset or something like that. I'm not quite sure how one would work out the vision bit, but it could be an interesting problem.

"Ping."

"An angel descended with some tablets from the Lord." Picture of angel zooming in for a perfect three-point landing with tablets strapped on his back.

"Ping."

SLAM. Anyway, the baby laughed.

"The trouble is," he said, "the colour of the wall detracts from the colour of the canvas." Watch your step, buddy, I mixed that colour myself.

"Well," said Margaret, "I'm afraid I don't see where else we can hang it. But I do agree, the wall doesn't do justice to it. Are you sure you want us to have it?" Careful, Margaret, always look directly at the person to whom you are speaking.

"Of *course* he wants you to have it," said the haunted wife. "And if it's worth something some day, you deserve it for encouraging him." We'd deserve it for looking at it.

We all sat down for tea. I looked at the twins uneasily.

"They don't seem very happy on the sofa. Perhaps they'd like to sit on the floor?" They sat on the sofa. What the hell, it's the landlady's sofa and maybe they only react to wood. The huge canvas loomed over us. Portrait of an Unfortunate Tortilla.

"I haven't named it yet," he said. "It seems to detract from the canvas to give it a name. Limits one's aesthetic reaction, or channels it, I should say."

"He never signs his pictures," the wife confided to Margaret. I should bloody well hope not.

"We have a remark-ay-ble new mascara stick," confided Mrs. Pilkinson, helping herself to another sausage roll. "It not only colours the lashes, but tiny filaments in the colouring agent make the lashes longer than they really are. It comes in forest green, Mediterranean blue, sunset mauve and jungle brown."

"Ping."

Picture of Mrs. Pilkinson leaving our fine little rented house with bulging tummy and full order book. When Margaret looks at me I tell her she resembles a whisk broom.

The earnest young man takes out a little black notebook.

"And shall we put down June thirtieth as the date of your total immersion?" Stunned silence.

"I'm afraid," says the voice of the serpent, "that there's been a misunderstanding."

"Ping."

"Then you wouldn't give your child a transfusion even if it were dying?"

"The Bible says we must eat no blood."

"They usually give it to you in the arm, my friend, not in a teacup."

He wants his magazines back.

"I gave them to the baby. She's teething again. There's nothing in the Bible that says you can't eat newsprint, is there?"

"Ping" and Fade Out.

"Mrs. Pilkinson, my wife is lying down."

"Well, I'll just nip in and—"

"No, you won't just nip in and—Mrs. Pilkinson, this is a small house. There is only one chest of drawers, Mrs. Pilkinson. The chest of drawers is already full of your products and there is no room for my underwear." I move closer. "As you know from my wife, Mrs. Pilkinson, I do not use a deodorant. And because I do not use a deodorant I need to have a large supply of underpants and vests. If I have to cut down I'll get *smelly*. You wouldn't want me to get smelly, would you, Mrs. Pilkinson?" I move one step closer.

"Ping. Ping. Ping."

"So I will just fit this piece of muslin over the intake-hole and away we go." The vacuum cleaner pries into all the secrets of the sofa, runs along the carpet and up the walls. He dumps a large amount of dirt on the landlady's flowered carpet.

"You look like a decent clean-living young couple. Now can you sit there and tell me you want that pretty baby of yours to grow up in all this *filth*?"

"Yes. And I'll thank you to clean up that mess you made before you leave."

"Ping."

Hermann opens the boot and stands back as though he is about to show us the crown jewels.

"Well. Well. That *is* interesting, Hermann. Ah—are you going to do some sculpture on the side?"

"You do not recognize it?"

"Well, to be honest with you, Hermann, I don't." He beams and struggles to pull the immense block of stone onto the lawn.

"Here, Hermann, let me help you with that." Oh God, it's some sort of present. Cornerstone from a building he blew up single-handed. Where in hell are we going to put it?

"Thank you. I am not so strong as once I was."

The three of us stand there and Margaret practices appreciative noises in her throat.

"You do not understand? Good. I have gone into business for myself. I have decided the only way to succeed in this country is to go into business for oneself. You notice the finish?"

The blank surface of the stone catches the last rays of the sun.

"Well, it's very shiny. You must have been working hard to get it so shiny." I knew he'd go crazy in the end. Poor guy. My heart goes out to Hermann the German and his crazy block of stone.

"Ha," remarks Hermann slyly. "I did not polish her. She polishes herself!" Then we lift the stone back into the boot and Hermann carefully covers it over with old rags.

"Morpheus Memorial Markers," says Hermann, striding toward the door with energy and purpose in every step. "Morpheus Memorial Markers. You like it—no?"

Hermann eats the last chocolate-chip cookie. "You see, my friends, many years ago I had given to me a secret formula for cast concrete. 'So what,' you will say, 'cast concrete has been around for a long time.' But have you ever heard of the cast concrete which *polishes herself*?"

We hadn't.

"It looks like granite, the stone?"

It looked like granite.

"Well, I decided to get some samples made up and now I am no longer the man from Transatlantic, I am Morpheus Memorial Markers. You like the name?" This addressed to Margaret—one poet to another.

"Very suitable."

"The classical reference, the alliteration—the Canadians will eat it up."

"How many have you sold so far, Hermann?"

"Well, that is the trouble. The stones I can get made, but I need a chiseller. At a reasonable price. The stones I have arranged. The chiseller I have still to arrange."

"You mean a man who will chisel the epitaphs?"

"That is it."

"Margaret has a friend who's an artist. I could give you his address."

"He's a painter, dear. What makes you think he could use a chisel?"

"I'm sure he could use a chisel a damn sight better than he can use a paintbrush. Anyway, it's worth a try if Hermann wants somebody cheap. And look how clever he is at carpentry—building that cabin and those potty-chairs and all that." I give him the address.

"Say, Hermann, how much are these memorial markers going to sell for?"

"I had thought of $49.95. The Canadians, they like the 95." He looks at us wistfully. "I don't suppose you'd care to...?"

"Well, Hermann, unless I get fat on all this baking Margaret does, or murder somebody, or something like that, I don't think I'll be needing one of those for a long time. But it's a great idea, Hermann, really great. I guess you'll be pretty busy from now on—getting the new business started up and so forth."

"I am never so busy as to neglect my friend and his charming wife. Besides, there is the Book."

"Oh, yes," (foiled again by Hermann-never-take-a-hint), "of course, there's the book."

"I suppose we could have kept it in the garage."

"Next to the painting?"

"Ping."

95

We stood in the bathtub and waited for the footsteps to die away.

"Are you there, my friends? My friends, are you in there?" (Oh no you don't, Hermann. Not this time.) "Please, my friends, I am desperate. I wish to use your bathroom."

We step gracefully, and in unison, over the rim.

"Well, Hermann. This is a surprise. Margaret was just scrubbing my back." (What in hell is he wearing? Been to a masquerade or something?) "We thought you had forgotten us."

"Excuse me, please, for one minute." A Hermann resplendent in gold braid goes quickly into the bathroom and shuts the door. Margaret yawns delicately and puts the coffee on.

"What is he wearing?"

"Don't worry, we'll soon find out."

"I am sorry to trouble you, my friends. I am now commissionaire at the Olympia. Until business is better. You like the uniform, no?"

"Terrific, Hermann." (Why, you poor bastard, won't they even let you take a pee on the house?)

Margaret comes in with coffee and tomorrow's breakfast rolls.

"You look wonderful, Hermann. And you've lost weight, haven't you?"

"You think so?" Hermann beams and takes off his hat with the patent leather visor. I switch the recorder on.

"Did I ever tell you of how the Italians became our servants?"

"No, you didn't."

"Well, at Corinth there were always about four, five thousand Italian prisoners, plus the Greeks, in the same barracks. They were supposed to be released. But for some unknown reason, the Germans didn't release them. So they were supposed to be free, but were still prisoners. Both of us were prisoners you might say...."

No, Hermann, we can't ping you. I put my arm around Margaret while the tape recorder whirrs on. . . and on. . . and on. . . .

ONE IS ONE & ALL ALONE

On the third day she rose reluctantly, deliberately ignoring the knocks until the last possible face-saving moment.

"Cock-cock-cock-cock-cock." An absurd form of onomatopoeia, or a deferential rooster. "Cock-cock-cock-cock."

"Yes, all right, I'm awake."

"Six-tirty, Madame."

"Thank you. I'm just getting up now." She wanted to shout, "*Thirty*, you silly bastard, thirty! Six-thirty." But his sandals were already slapping self-righteously down the stairs—slap-slap-slap, a reproof to her laziness. "And guess-slap-slap-how-slap-long-slap-we-slap-have been up-slap slap." He moved off toward the kitchen as she sat there, her head bowed, like one about to take up a heavy burden. The children were already awake and she could hear them giggling and fighting in the far bedroom. Two days, two nights already over—only twelve nights to go.

Only twelve nights. She took up an eyebrow pencil and carefully crossed out another date on the small calendar above the dressing table. "Brighton, 'The Lanes.'" It looked so cool, the picture. Cool and safe. Once they had gone around the Lanes and she had seen a Victorian dolls' house in a window—a beautiful thing, and she longed to reach out and touch it, to own it. "That's lovely," she said, and her husband, amused, "For yourself or Baby? Isn't she a bit young?" And they had laughed and moved on, she glancing back once, over her shoulder. A whim—but it had been lovely. It looked—what was the saying?—safe. "Safe as houses." She would have liked to live in a solid, square, beautifully ugly house like that. Safe, ugly, beautiful and cool. "You're being romantic," said her heavy-eyed reflection in the mirror. "Ah no," she waggled her finger severely at this other woman. "If I were romantic I should like it here. Colour, light, eternal summer—and servants. *I* am not romantic—somebody else is," she muttered darkly to the other woman, then slammed the top down hard, and smiled.

After breakfast, with the older child safely on her way to the bus (but *will* she be safe, wasn't she a little flushed, should she have worn a cardigan against the damp, would she remember to look both ways?), she played with the littler until the nursery bus came. The child had been drawing happily, head down in concentration. "Don't look," she cried and snuggled the paper to her when her mother came near. "It's a surprise." Then the bus had honked and the child had run off, screwing the drawing up and thrusting it into her pocket.

"What have you drawn? Can't Mummy see?"

"No, no. It's a surprise for my teacher."

She had returned, a little hurt, to the house. Already then, they were going away, even the youngest. Six months ago it would have been a surprise for *her*, would have been brought carefully for her to inspect, to approve, to shower praise upon. Now it was for "teacher." "I should accept it and rejoice," she told herself sternly. "They are independent—outgoing. That is what we want." But it was hard. "Children don't break away," she reflected, "not if they are healthy. They glide away like skaters. A few wobbly steps and they're off." "But unaware of the thin ice," she cried to that other woman, "unaware of the sprains, the strains." And she, so aware, so ultimately responsible—she must keep still. Mothers should be seen and not heard. Look what had happened to her, an emotional cripple skating on artificial legs—skillfully, yes—so skillfully that no-one was aware, except her husband, that the performance was done with such a handicap, that she ached at times with the strain of being "normal" and unhysterical. Her mother's voice—"Watch out, you'll fall." "Don't do that, you might hurt yourself." Sitting in a car with her head darting from side to side. "Slow down." "Watch out for that car," to her father, driving. And so she had never broken a bone or climbed a high tree or run out in front of traffic. Always safe—and always afraid. She wondered sometimes why her children did not sense the fear which lurked, like a ground-fog, around their mother; why they didn't smell it—as animals are said to sense and smell fear in a human being. The wages of fear is death, too. She had known this now, for several years. Only this death wasn't sudden: it crept up slowly, softly, cat-like, waiting to pounce in the still hours of the night and shake her by the throat. At first she had hated her mother, when she realized what had happened; then pitied her; then hated herself for pitying one with so little self-control. Yet now, in this place, as she felt herself cracking, her own control melting under the heat of the tropics and the dangers which lay in wait for her here, now her pity had returned. She wondered suddenly if her mother would have been happier here—if the damp and snow of New England had had a disastrous effect upon *her*, just as she now sweated and strained to remain upright in the heat. And she thought again of Brighton and the Lanes. Yet she knew, in her heart, that this was not so—that the weak carry their weakness with them wherever they go, like a tramp with his clothes done up on the end of a stick. The heat simply exposed her for what she was—her mother's daughter—weak and afraid. She remembered grimly the quarrels they—she and her husband—had overheard, lying in bed and sweating, louvres wide open to catch any passing breeze, quarrels between couples who, on the surface, would appear never to quarrel. And the drinking, the endless parties, the sudden shouting at servants (or children), the gossip which spread, literally, like fire across the heat-struck compound. "Beat the heat." She had seen that often enough in advertisements back home. "Beat the heat." Here the heat beat them. The sun, a child's drawing, bristling with rays, and each ray a whip which beat them all until they were bruised and sore, and tempers flared, little pettinesses opened into gaping wounds.

She thought of the wooden figures upstairs in the spare room, so carefully collected, so laboriously bargained for by her husband, sitting cross-legged on the verandah opposite the trader in his long white smock and little cap. They would sit there sometimes for an hour, the old man patient and shrewd, her husband, contented, turning a figure or a mask slowly in his large, competent hands. "Name your last price," and he, refusing to commit himself until he was sure the old man was ready to bargain. "Name your last price," and gradually, the old man's price would go down, her husband's price would go up, and the figure would change hands, or, no price acceptable to both, the old man would roll everything up in rags, the crocodile skins, the gold weights, the ugly highly polished faces that looked as though they were turned out in a factory, and the one or two really good things. An enormous bundle of the good and the bad, hoisted on the head of the porter, who had sat silent, smoking or eating kola nuts, glad to rest his back and lean against the cool concrete wall of the verandah.

The figures: most of them had cracked during this hot dry weather and it gave her a certain satisfaction to think that the wood, indigenous as it was, also, like her, suffered under the heat. Yet the figures were beautiful, and their cracks revealed nothing sinister—nothing was released from their depths that was not there on the surface. "Name your last price," she whispered to herself, as she sat over a second cup of coffee. But who would bargain for her? Who would sit patiently and turn her slowly in his hands, and finally agree to terms? Not God certainly—and not the devil. Not as she was now. She wondered suddenly if her husband, seeing her lately with all her cracks exposed, felt that he had got a bad bargain. A cracked figure was one thing—a cracked wife quite another. She had seen him look at her once or twice, she was sure, as though she were a stranger. ("And how many times has he looked that way and I have not seen him?") Had he resigned himself, like the Hausa Man's porter—she played with the image, once again—to carrying her, however heavy she might be, however grotesque, however much he might suspect that she was rubbish, setting her down gently when he could—for the sake of a rest in the shade and a cigarette? She had wept once that she was not like the other wives, could not play tennis in the sun or spend a lazy hour at the swimming pool, that she was tired, so tired. "It doesn't matter," he had said, "it doesn't matter." But it did. And now that she was worse, begged off from trips to towns or the movies, refused, in fact, to go out at all if she could avoid it, what did he think of his precious bargain now? ("But does he know what an effort it all is, how I do it to save him the embarrassment of having the cracks appear, with a little ripping sound, in public; that I do it quite literally to save face—his and mine?")

For there had been incidents, only one or two, but enough to frighten her, when the cracks *had* appeared in public, when, in another few minutes, if he had not extracted her, swiftly and skillfully, she might conceivably have "gone to pieces," like one of those animated cartoon figures that get hit on the head and still stand for a moment before they come crashing down in little bits. Once, in the Old Market, with friends, she had been closed in, encircled by black sweating faces, each urging her to buy a live fowl, hanging head-down, feet tied together; she couldn't stand it and fought her way out, running wildly through the muddy lanes looking for an exit, a way out. He had caught up with her, found a path which led to the outside, walked with her, his arm steady under her shaking elbow, and gone back later to explain to the friends, though what he had said she never knew. And she had not gone to the market again; next time he went alone. A wife and a companion. He would have been better off with a faithful dog! ("And now the distance between my house and the friendly gap in my neighbour's hedge is as terrifying to me as a journey across a dark and crocodile-infested river.") Yet he had left her alone. Alone and not alone, with two children to care for and a servant to direct. Was this, then, some kind of test? Was it, in fact, a final attempt to make her face up to things, to "cope"? Yet the children were at school all morning, and the old man who washed and cooked and cleaned needed, really, no direction from her except a quick suggestion as to lunch and dinner. A very easy test—or was it? Wasn't she already afraid, already beginning to crack and only two days gone? ("And a child can break a leg, be bitten by a snake, get malaria—or worse. Old Samuel can start talking back, or thieving things or just walk off into the bush.") The world was made in seven days—surely her world could be unmade in twelve. She got up hastily and took her cup out to the kitchen. "Samuel." Where was he? Again, "Samuel." "Madame?" from upstairs. And she had not even heard him go up; he must have seen her sitting there, have passed the table and smiled, possibly with contempt, at the young Madame talking to her coffee cup. She heard him come to the top of the stairs—slip-slap-slip-slap. "You call me, Madame?"

"Nothing. It doesn't matter. What are you doing?"

"Change beds, Madame. We always change beds on Tuesdays." Genuine reproach in his voice—or was he mocking her? ("Why *we*? And who decided Tuesdays? Why do we change beds on Tuesdays? A ridiculous day to change beds." Surely it hadn't been *her* idea.)

"Samuel." ("And if I ask him will he tell me?") "Never mind."

"Yes, Madame." Slip-slap-slip-slap—he went back down the hall.

And when she suggested grilled cheese sandwiches for lunch he stood there, his head on one side. "Laura, she say she want baked beans, and the Baby she want fried egg and fried bread." She fought back tears of frustration.

"The children are not to give you orders, they know that."

"It's all right, Madame."

"It's *not* all right. We'll have grilled cheese sandwiches."

"Yes, Madame." And when neither child finished her sandwich, he took the plates away without comment, ignoring their accusing looks.

By tea time the sun had disappeared and the sky was swollen with dark clouds, like huge blisters about to burst. Yet it was still hot; and she let the children play in the bath, while she washed her long hair and tried to get cool. She stuck her head directly under the tap and let the tepid water run over her scalp until she became giddy and had to hold onto the basin as she reached with one hand for a dry towel. Afterward she patted the children dry and let them try on lipstick and nail polish. (As penance for her behaviour over the lunch.) They stood in front of the long mirror admiring their new sophistication—straight-limbed, glossy-haired, the littlest adorned with necklaces of shells.

"How do you do Mrs. Ahlorabee?" the little one said to her sister's reflection. The older girl giggled, watching her lips open and shut, wrapped in her own particular dream. How many more years before they would stand thus, aware of themselves in a new way, dusting their armpits with talc, tingling in anticipation of the evening? Seven, eight for the elder perhaps. Their bodies interested them now as intricate pieces of machinery—not much more. Of their hearts—the complex set of signals which would set their blood racing at the sight of a particular face, the sound of special laughter —they knew nothing. Just so must Eve have admired herself in one of the many pools of Eden, a sexless, almost aesthetic reaction.

"Do they bury you with your clothes on?" Like a clap of thunder. She stood in the doorway and the small voice seemed to come to her from a distance. ("Careful now. Careful.")

"Yes. Of course."

"But what if you die in the bath?" ("Are they being infected then, already, by my own morbid fears—my imagination?" She saw her mind as a great swamp out of which rose the pestilential damps of her anxieties. And the children breathed it in—all of it—and brought forth questions.)

"Then they have to dress you. But nobody's going to die in the bath, in this house. Shall we go down and have a cool drink?"

"Two straws. May I have two straws?"

"Yes, yes," she promised, dressing them quickly. "Two straws." Her relief made her weak. It was only a casual question after all, something to say—something to shock perhaps. But on the way downstairs, the elder. . . "Do they take your ring off before they bury you?"

"Of course not." She saw her hand, fleshless, the finger-

105

nails long and curling inward, and the gold band, loose now, winking triumphantly up at her; became terribly aware of bones, hers and theirs—bones descending the staircase—the small bones of her children holding carefully to the railing, three skeletons with long hair wandering aimlessly through a deserted house. And old Samuel, his bones as white as theirs, chopping onions, for their supper, in the kitchen.

And still the rain held off. They ate their supper and she was reading the children a story when the first flashes of lightning arced across the sky.

"Soo-oop of the e-e-evening," she said resolutely. "Beautiful, beautiful soup!" Then there was a terrible crash, somewhere near the houses on the Ridge, and the lights went out.

"Samuel," she called, "Samuel!" The children whimpered, the oldest, from somewhere in the darkness beside her, "Please, Mummy, I don't want candles."

"No candles." The other took up the cry.

"Don't be so silly. The candles won't hurt you."

"I'm afraid. The house will burn down."

Samuel appeared with a lighted candle, his hand and face grotesque, distorted in the flickering light. He looked horrible, savage. ("Don't be so silly," she said to herself. "It's Samuel.")

The children whimpered again as she took a candle and lit it. Her hand shook, and she felt, rather than saw, this new, savage-eyed Samuel look at her in surprise.

"Thank you Samuel. Take a candle for yourself and leave one here on the coffee table. Then you may go." She wanted him out, away, in his own quarters at the back of the house. She was afraid of him. ("And he knows it, he's laughing at me.") She hurried the weeping children up the stairs, her light casting crazy shadows on the walls. Twice the thunder cracked as she fumbled for their pyjamas, brushed their teeth, tucked them in bed. The younger was howling with fear and the elder lay silent and shaking—which was worse.

"I'll put the candle in the hall, shall I?—and then you'll have some light."

"No. Take it away. I don't mind the dark."

Helpless. "You mustn't be afraid."

"The house will burn down." (And where had she gotten this idea? Who had frightened the child with such stories? She was angry now—at the child and at the unknown person who had told her God knows what terrible tale of burning houses.)

"Listen," she said desperately, "the house won't burn down and I don't want to hear such rubbish."

"It could."

"It couldn't. Most of it is concrete."

"The doors aren't. The stairs aren't. The floors aren't."

Helpless again. "Well, it won't burn."

"Houses do."

"Not this house." (How do you comfort them—with lies or half-truths only? How could she, her mother's daughter, defeat the logic of this child?)

The thunder cracked and a great flash of lightning illuminated the little room. She saw them suddenly as though they were actors in a play: the two children awaiting her cue and she, inexperienced, an understudy shoved suddenly in front of the footlights—the right words forgotten or never known. She blew the candle out.

"Don't be afraid." Willing them to accept, to cease questioning. "The candle is out and thunder and lightning won't hurt you."

"Lightning could fire the house."

Triumphant. "No, it couldn't. We have lightning rods."

"What are lightning rods?"

"You know, Daddy showed you. Those two poles at the ends of the house. If the lightning comes near it will run down those metal poles and into the earth."

"Is that the truth?"

"That's the truth." Yet she sat with them until they went to sleep, willing herself not to jump, while the thunder boomed its terrible, apocalyptic cry across the dark night and the sky flickered on and off like fire. There had been two huge chestnut trees in front of their house when she was a child, and now she heard her mother's voice call out, "Come away from the sitting-room. Those trees might crash against the house." She would be afraid to go to bed, and would lie, wide-eyed and panic-stricken, the pillow over her head, until the storm subsided and she fell into a restless sleep. Would she have lain thus, without the fear in her mother's voice? Possibly. Probably. Who knows? So now she sat still until her legs ached, willing herself not to jump, never to call out, not to kindle the already smouldering fears of her own children—as though she herself were lightning and could strike them at will. When she was satisfied that they would not wake up, she slipped off her sandals and walked barefoot down the hall to her own room, hers and her husband's, and undressed in the dark. The rain beat down on the metal roof with impatient, masculine fingers. Drum—drum, come, come now, hurry up. The dry earth sucked and squirmed under the pressure of the storm. Wait for me oh wait there there touch me there and there and there yes oh yes. She lay naked on the big bed listening to the rain, waiting for the earth to be satisfied, to transmit to her some of its coolness, its strength. Once she had made love behind a waterfall, scrambling down the cliff, afraid to look below but drawn on down and down, by the power of the boy beside her. There was a bed of rock, wet, cool to the touch; and they had undressed quickly, joyously, the great curtain of water in front of them quivering, urging them to hurry. Afterward, they had lain in each other's arms, eyes closed, as though in a great, grey-green sack—unborn again —triumphant in their youth and nakedness. And now? Would she, even if asked, scramble down such a cliff, even for such a joy as she had felt that afternoon? Knowledge is fear. She whimpered softly into her solitary pillow and fell asleep.

By Friday there were four large crosses on the calendar and she felt quite calm. The air was hot and dry again and the sky a merciless blue; yet the storm had given her strength, a second wind, as it were, and the strange female world into which she had been plunged was becoming more familiar. Samuel was Samuel once again and not the savage she had glimpsed that night. She gave her few orders quietly and firmly and he went about the house as usual. She had discovered that she did not have to leave the house if she did not choose, for her husband had stocked up well before he left. She read late and went back to bed after the children had left for school, rising refreshed before lunch and playing with the children until their rest. This morning she had smiled shyly at the woman in the mirror. "You see? I'm not such a bad sort after all." She even toyed with the idea of getting someone to take her into town, buying some material, having her hair done. "Why can't you drive yourself?" the woman in the mirror had said, rather sternly. "It isn't as though he had taken the car." But she shrugged her shoulders ("You know why") and refused to become involved or irritated. She saw herself in a new dress, hair coiled prettily on her head, going to open the door. And her husband, surprised, delighted, proud of her. Yet when her neighbour came over and offered her a lift she decided against it, gave her some money for eggs and remembered that she had the mending to do. No use in going too fast. Like someone who has just discovered that water will hold him up, she was a bit uncertain about going too far out of her depth in case her courage—or the water—betrayed her. She made some ice cream for tea, and cupcakes, bustling about importantly, joking with Samuel, getting in his way.

"What do you think, Samuel? Will they like that?" She had finished icing the cakes and was licking the spoon.

"Very nice, Madame."

"They're good girls, Samuel."

"Very good girls, Madame." She was very proud of them suddenly, swollen-eyed with pride that they had been, *were* indeed, very good girls. Her girls, and very good.

They were all quite merry at tea, which they had on the verandah as a special treat. Samuel had found a jar of peanut butter high up in the store room and offered this to her shyly as his contribution to the party. And there was a dish of groundnuts, newly roasted. The sun was sullen, unwilling to relinquish its hold to the waiting night; but today she did not mind, sat, even, facing the garden with its silent green explosions, the gigantic sisal plants, the red hibiscus flowers like fresh blood, which clung to the hedge separating her house from her neighbour's. Soon bath, story time, another day safely over, her frail craft and its cargo sailing serenely toward the dark. And she, captain, the wheel in her frail, firm hands, guiding them, guiding herself as well, carefully, gently toward the end of the journey, the day when her husband was due to return.

As if reading her thoughts, or part of them, the younger:

"Where is he now, Mummy?"

"Right up at the border. Tomorrow they start coming down."

"Will he bring us presents?" The elder.

"If you're good."

"And you as well." The younger, guttural with peanut butter.

"I expect so."

"If you're good." ("Touché," she thought. "But you're wrong. He always brings me presents—beautiful pots, baskets, a curious necklace—and himself.")

"Aren't I always good?"

"Sometimes you smack us." (The elder, grave, green-eyed, determined never to smack her children—oh no!)

"That's not because *I* have been naughty." She grabbed a handful of groundnuts and the three of them chewed thoughtfully.

That was when her filling came out. A nasty crunch, and her hand, suddenly, to her mouth.

"What's the matter?"

She ran to the toilet and spat into her hand. There it was, dull grey, ominous. ("Oh no! Why me?") She explored the hole cautiously with her tongue. The nerve jumped, struck out at her like a claw. She flushed the mess down the toilet and washed her hands. The children had come in, anxious.

"It's only a filling," she said weakly. "Mummy bit down on the groundnuts and her filling came out."

"Will you have to go to the dentist?" Curious, not really sympathetic, not *their* catastrophe. The room swayed.

"No," she said weakly. "I don't think so."

"*I* had to go. Twice." The elder opened her mouth wide and pointed to a gap and a filling.

"Well, perhaps I shall have to go. We'll see."

"My teacher says if you get a hole in your tooth you should tell your Mummy and Daddy right away and go to the dentist."

"All right. Let's drop the subject." ("Shut up, shut up. I don't want to go. I won't go. It's going to be all right.")

But of course it wasn't. As though she had turned over a stone and released some nasty, stinging creature, the sore tooth jumped and writhed until her jaw, her ear, her neck were on fire with the pain. Unable to sleep, she watched the shipwreck of her good intentions, pacing the upstairs hall in her bare feet, gazing resentfully at the dark windows of the compound, sleeping.

"Why me?" she cried again. "Why me?" And if she ran to her neighbours on either side, threw herself on their mercy, exclaimed and explained that she hated dentists, hated pain, was unable to cope any longer, what would they say, rubbing sleep from their astonished eyes, surveying her wild hair, her nightgown, her bare feet? Comfort?

"It's all right. We understand. It doesn't matter." Pitying her, but condemning her, yes; the women with their cheerful faces and uncomplicated minds, the men sighing with relief that she wasn't, after all, their responsibility.

She switched on the bathroom light and stood counting out pills in her hand. She had promised ("but only myself") that she would take one a day, no more. Pretty things, black and turquoise, like small gift parcels from some exclusive shop. How many were there—fifteen, twenty, thirty? It was unfair that they should have given her more than a week's supply—such a temptation, such a responsibility. Yet, it would be so easy; they were not difficult to swallow. She could lie down and rest, triumph over the pain of the aching tooth, all the accumulated pains which tore at her, stripped away her masks. Triumph over the woman in the mirror, too—shut her mouth once and for all. But who would explain, who would understand? The children, running in, finding her cold and still. What would they think, tomorrow, ten years from now, twenty? Samuel, who could neither read nor write, shuffling to the neighbours, his head on one side, embarrassed, ashamed to be the servant of one who was not herself a master? Who would tell her husband? Wouldn't he feel it was all his fault, that he never should have gone? ("Well, you shouldn't have gone. It is your fault! Who else but you would have the innocence, the faith, the *nerve* to leave two defenceless children—yours after all, as well as mine—in the hands of a mad woman?") She began to cry, to whimper. What was the use of pretending any more?

The next morning, after the children had gone to school, she carefully backed the car up the twisting drive and made her way to the university clinic.

"No," she said to the young doctor who glanced at her puffy eyes and swollen cheek with concern, "it's nothing serious. Just a filling that came out. Can you give me something for the pain?"

"I can give you a letter to the hospital. You take it there and they will make an appointment. If it is so swollen, it will probably have to come out."

"I don't want it out. I mean," she managed a laugh, "I'm getting to the stage where I've got to hang on to as many teeth as possible. I'm sure my dentist at home can do something." The doctor was both amused and angry.

"When are you due for leave?"

"The first of July."

"And now it is the end of May. My dear lady!"

"Well, I must wait until my husband returns and discuss the matter with him."

He made a sweeping gesture.

"But there is nothing to discuss. If the tooth is abscessed it must come out. If not, they will fill it. We do have trained dentists here, you know."

The pain made her giddy, and her smile, this time, came out as a grimace.

"Of course. I didn't mean to imply they were butchers or anything like that." Her knees were shaking; soon she would have to sit down. "It's just something that must be discussed when my husband is here."

"And when is your husband expected?"

"Nine days' time."

He smiled at her, one adult to another.

"Nine days' time! You can't go around like that for nine days." Then he looked at her closely. She saw him only as a dark, whirling shape—a menace. "Is something wrong? The pills you were given, they do not relax you?"

"Wrong?" she moaned. Her voice seemed thin as wire and far away. "No, nothing's wrong."

Then the nerve jumped again and, surprised, he caught her as she fell.

It was nearly dark when the airplane finally arrived and fog had already smudged the landscape. A night, he thought, for Manet; not for Whistler and his Nocturnes, but for someone who knew how to smear, blear, recreate the tension and noise of a place of arrival and departure. Depressionism, if you like—a night for a depressionist painter, a night like a charcoal sketch grown grey with age and neglect.

The waiters waited, in various attitudes of apathy or impatience, for the plane was late. Tables in town were sitting forlorn with "Reserved" signs on them; dinners in the suburbs were being kept warm over boiling water; lovers, husbands, wives, businessmen, all were suspended, waiting, because a piece of tin no bigger than a toy as yet and containing the loved ones—wives, husbands, colleagues of those behind the barrier and those behind anxious doors— a piece of tin, a toy, was, had been, powerless against the fog. His parents, too, would be waiting, would have already driven, probably, to meet one, two trains—annoyed, disgusted (his father), anxious, grim-faced (his mother)— having eaten hurriedly if at all and wondering in their heart of hearts, or perhaps out loud by this time, how it had ever come to this.

Yet in spite of his reverie (or perhaps because of?) he saw her first, not hurrying, looking neither left nor right as though sure of his presence even though she knew, must know, he had been waiting four hours, standing around, hungry, tired, fingers stained yellow from too many half-smoked cigarettes. He watched her progress slyly, hardly shifting his position, merely turning his head slightly, casually, to the right, as an assassin might pin-point his victim in a crowd. She had on a coat he had not seen before, flaring, low-belted in the back, of some mauve and black mixture. She also wore a hat and that startled him, made her look younger somehow—a black velvet Garboesque affair, with one side pulled back to reveal her face. "She dresses well," he thought, and then, "Mother won't like that." How he knew he did not know, but he was certain that the new fashionable coat, the large black hat, would be met with polite, but furious, frozen disapproval, as though somehow she were not keeping her part of the bargain, were not *grateful* enough perhaps? She looked too well, too self-possessed. Should he warn her, coach her, rehearse the meeting on the way up, explain the inexplicable unspoken rules and regulations which she had already, if not exactly violated, at least infringed upon, by her obvious health and well-being? And, of course, the new coat and hat. Her mother, last week, on the phone, no doubt meaning him to overhear (if not consciously, then unconsciously, as most of a woman's work seemed to be carried on or out): "No, we've decided no holiday this year, what with one thing and another. There it is, it can't be helped. Oh a week in Brighton, perhaps, but not to the Continent—we can't afford it." And now the new coat and hat. He felt his stomach turn over. Nothing would be said of course; nothing really had been since the one, the Faustian scene. But everything would be implied, hinted at. They both, she particularly, would be attacked subtly, politely, would be stung before she knew what had happened. He went forward and touched her arm, then wordlessly took the baggage checks from her outstretched hand and

116

they walked away, her arm rigid under his hand, toward the waiting bus.

Yet it was only when they were on the train, he honour-bound to find an empty compartment although his whole being yearned for company, for crowds, for anything but the awful responsibility of at last being alone with her; it was only when they had found an empty compartment and her cases had been stacked above them, the torn baggage checks lolling over the edge like tongues, and she took off her coat, folding it neatly, lining side out, that the reason for her being there, the reason for his waiting four hours at the airport, sank in, or if you like, down, as though he had swallowed a stone. My god, she was big; the coat, the wide-flaring, fashionable coat which was bound to cause trouble sooner or later, was an excellent disguise, allowing her to travel incognito, under false colours as it were. He was shocked, as though he had witnessed something obscene, a caricature, a grotesque parody. At any moment pillows would drop out or balloons would deflate with a nasty "fffr" and she would be standing there, flat-stomached, the dress hanging loosely around her slim hips, and she laughing, bold as brass—"Did I frighten you?" The mere physical fact of her sitting there, like that, hands (which in contrast looked incredibly small, as though they had been painted onto her lap as a hasty and not-too-successful afterthought) folded, serene, smug perhaps, in such a place revolted and terrified him.

"Did you have a nice flight?" His voice was loud, came out as an accusation, not a question.

"It was all right." She stared hard at him, forcing him to return her gaze, and when he did something flickered between them; unknown, terrible, not to be encouraged, allowed to grow.

"I don't like planes," she said. Then, more to herself than to him, "So shut in—confined with a lot of people one doesn't know."

"You can always look out the windows." Making sounds, small talk, smaller than small—simply indicating that he was listening.

"Oh yes," she said, "and see what you're passing by." She made a pillow from her coat and leaned against it, and with a gesture as final as a royal dismissal, she waved her hand slowly in his direction and closed her eyes. He sat looking at the, to him, blank pages of his book and wondering if, in fact, it could have turned out any other way.

At Watford Junction a woman and baby entered their compartment. He felt a rush of relief. In the presence of a third person perhaps they could both relax. The girl never opened her eyes, but he knew both that she had not been asleep and that she had seen and accepted, also with relief, the woman and child. The woman was tired, visibly so, with dark smudges under her eyes and the dirty complexion of the Midlands, a face that reminded him of wet pavements and soot-soiled factory windows. Her hair in rollers underneath a faded scarf. Chilblains too, rubbing the heel of one foot with the toes of the other. The baby whimpered and she rummaged absently in her string bag until she found a dummy and stuck it in the child's mouth. She propped the baby against her and opened a *Woman's Mirror*, plunging swiftly into the enchanted world where true love, however harassed, wins out always and you, too, can look like our December model for only two pounds and a little effort.

For whom, for what, would she unroll her hair tonight? Her husband, in his stocking feet, reading the Pool's winners with his elbows on the table, reaching absent-mindedly for HP sauce, grunting a "yes" or "no" as she moved around the kitchen? Or tonight—payday—would they leave the baby with an older child, an aunt, the mother-in-law, and go around the corner to the local where he would play darts and drink pint after pint, she sipping what—gin and orange? Babycham?—whatever working-class wives sip as they sit at tables in the smoky rooms, exchanging gossip with the neighbourhood wives. No, it would be too late for all that by the time the train got in, assuming, of course, that she was going as far as he, they, but even if not, she had the stamp of a longish journey about her, a "settled" look if that was the right way of putting it.

Perhaps she simply put in the rollers from force of habit, was unaware, even, that they were there, little sausage-looking lumps under the head scarf, and would leave them in all night. He tried to imagine what it would be like to sleep with a woman who wore her hair in rollers. Reach out to touch your beloved and find Medusa instead, snakes all coiled up and having a snooze on your (technically anyway) pillow. Was that real love, when all the barriers were down, the man scratched his balls with impunity, the woman wore rollers to bed? All the little, private acts of life which he had never considered before loomed suddenly ominous and important—the cutting of toenails, breaking wind, the desire to pick one's nose (and the sometimes conscious or absent-minded act itself), remembering to pull the chain. He looked carefully across at the girl, who seemed to be really asleep now, curled up with her face protected from the plush seat by the smooth silky lining of her coat. Would she ever wear rollers on a train—or to the market or to bed? He realized that he had spent nights with her and days with her, but never a string of nights and days; had never, in other words, lived with her. He knew she was untidy; her flat was always a jumble of paper and books and he had taken this (then) as a positive sign—that her work and zest for life meant more to her than the meaningless rituals of "straightening up" and "sorting out." She herself laughed about it, pointed out quickly to new acquaintances that she had no "powers of organization." Surely, examined now, this laughing self-acceptance of her own weakness indicated, hinted at, a major flaw? He had never examined her cupboards, looked for dust in the corners. But of course she *seemed* scrupulously clean in her person, carried about with her an aura, almost, of hot baths and talc and weekly shampoos. He knew she shaved her legs, for they were as smooth and hairless as a baby's, never a trace of stubble, there or underneath her arms. She had been amazed, she told him once, that so many English girls did not bother—even dark-haired ones. She thought it looked dirty, untidy. Something he had not particularly noticed until then. After that, whenever he had seen the dark curling hairs underneath sheer stockings, he had mentally agreed with her—dirty, untidy. But perhaps that was all part of the trap. Perhaps underneath her scrubbed innocence lay a slut, a woman who, having "caught" her man, would let herself go—wear rollers to bed, neglect or forget to change her underwear. Wasn't her attitude, now that he thought of it in this new light, rather cavalier? And was this too part of the trap—this bulge underneath the soft green pleats of her frock? Suddenly he felt that it was he, himself, who was in there, struggling and kicking to be free—trapped in a noose of silken thighs and sweet, deceptive darkness. She lay there asleep, cheeks cool against the silken splendour of her coat, relaxed. (For hadn't she got not only what she deserved but what she—he saw it now—wanted?) While he!

The train was beginning to slow down—Oxford, he supposed—and he thought for a minute of running out into the corridor and flinging himself off, losing himself amidst the spires and ancient stones, seeking sanctuary, leaving her and all that she implied travelling through the dark night. Something from a play, Shakespeare probably, though in a different context—if it were done when 'tis done, 'twere well it were done quickly. Something like that. When she woke up and found that he was gone, what would she do? He pictured her on the platform in her great, gay, swinging coat, his parents advancing to meet them—her. She, all alone. Bewildered, furious, in tears? What?

The baby began to cry again and she opened her eyes, turned her head so that she was facing him. For a moment she had the blank stare of a person who has awakened suddenly in a strange hotel room and can't remember where he is or why, has to orient himself to unfamiliar chests and cupboards, a door facing in the wrong direction. She stared stupidly at him, and then, as she felt the train slowing down, a look of such intense terror crossed her face that he thought she must be still asleep and dreaming. He reached out his hand and said in a low voice, "It's all right. Wake up. It's all right."

"Are we there? Is this the station?" Desperate, frantic eyes. The eyes of a trapped animal. He understood.

"No. I think it's Oxford. We've a long way yet—go back to sleep." She shivered and then sat up, rubbing her eyes hard with the backs of her fists. Then she pulled down her skirt and swivelled to peer out the window.

"Oxford. You're right." And she muttered to herself, as though it were a talisman, a magic formula, "A long while yet, a long while yet."

Footsteps up and down the corridor, voices, doors slamming. Faces peered in at them, saw, heard the crying baby and hurried on. Finally a middle-aged man, a traveller of some sort, peered, went away, came back, peered again and entered. He swung his sample-case up into the rack in a manner which suggested he'd had a successful trip.

"Should have taken the car, really," he said cheerfully to no-one in particular, more in order to establish, identify, himself, than anything else. "But all this rotten weather and the pile-ups on the M1 put me off." They nodded politely, even the roller-haired woman, who left off searching for something in order to recognize, establish that she recognized, the traveller as a man of property. He settled himself in the remaining corner, opposite the woman, opened the paper and deftly cut the end off a cigar. The woman had found what she was looking for, a digestive biscuit, and gave it to the baby, who sucked frantically for a few minutes, then quite literally dropped off to sleep, its head lolling stupidly against her, leaving bits of wet, mashed brown stuff on the worn blue jumper. He remembered some psychologist saying that man has a basic, never completely controlled desire to suck—hence mints, pipes, cigars and cigarettes. Pacifiers of a more sophisticated and acceptable kind. He looked down at his own stained fingers and wondered how many cigarettes he had smoked in the past four months. Too many. Or perhaps not enough—or the theory didn't work out in fact. He wasn't pacified.

The girl stood up suddenly, her face pale.

"Excuse me. I think I'll go out in the corridor for a few minutes." She opened the door as quietly as possible, so as not to wake the baby, and he followed her out.

"Is something the matter?" No answer. "Don't you feel well?" She stood with her face turned away from him, her cheek pressed against the damp window.

"I'll be all right in a minute, thank you." As though he were an overanxious stranger. Polite. Final.

He remembered, then, that she had travelled thousands of miles, had left God knew what transatlantic scene behind her, had another scene (most probably) ahead. Was now bumping across the English countryside, tired, possibly hungry, certainly shaken up both physically and mentally.

"Oh God," he thought, "she's going to have a miscarriage or something, here in the train." He tried to remember what one should do and realized there was nothing to remember —he didn't know, had never known. Something that happened to other people.

"It's the cigar," she said. "It makes me feel sick." Passed his hand across his forehead and realized he had been sweating.

"Do you want me to go back and ask him to put it out?"

She swung around abruptly. "And just what will you say?"

"What do you mean?"

"I mean how will you put it? Excuse me sir, my wife, that is my wife who is not my wife, the girl I am travelling with, is going to have a baby and your cigar, so obviously pleasurable to you, is making her feel sick." The words hung frozen, a wall of icicles between them.

"Don't," he said desperately. "Don't make it any worse than it is." She refrained from the obvious answer, the answer which occurred to him (and he cursed himself).

"Well, what would you say?" she insisted.

"I would say, 'Would you mind putting out your cigar,' and I would skip the cheap theatricals. If he's an understanding man, he'll put it out and that will be the end of it."

"The wonderful British reserve. Of course, I'd forgotten that."

"Don't," he pleaded again.

"Don't what? Don't be nasty? Don't make a public and therefore un-British scene? Don't worry about what people think? Look," she said, fumbling in her handbag. She opened her fist. "Thirty-nine cents in Woolworth's. My mother made me buy it. Would you like me to put it on?" She pressed her face once more against the window.

"Don't," he said, "don't." And always before it was do— do—do. And when it's done, it's don't do.

"She wants a scene," he thought, "—God knows she probably deserves one—" (one part of his mind said get it over with now before. . .) "but I'm tired and worried and want to sit down." He felt as though his knees were buckling under some tremendous weight. "Would you like to move to a different compartment?" (anything, only let me sit down) "I'll go down the corridor and find a non-smoker."

"No, we'd still have to go back and collect all our things. I told you I'd be all right in a minute. You can go back now."

"Don't you want me to stay with you?" The same words, used so often between them as a prelude, a password, sometimes a joke. She would say, "No," and lean against the door, one hand already taking the pins out of her hair until, suddenly released, it fell in great honey-coloured bunches, her eyes sparkling–glowing–the innocent temptress. Then she would bolt the door and turn off the lights. "No," she said now. And then, ungraciously, "I don't care." Silence— only the train muttering urgently to itself, calculating the number of miles accomplished, the number of miles to come. Back and forth they swayed, the rain silent and reproachful against the window. What was she thinking about? He hated her as one would hate an old lover met by chance many years later—the reality of his or her middle-age, false teeth, paunch, freckled hands destroying once and for all a cherished corner where he or she had remained immortal—exchanging honeyed kisses in the sun. He hated, then, this her, this creature beside him with the thin, frozen voice and the swollen body. This was what had happened to their dream-world, their arcadia. Come live with me and be my love. What fools they had been. This person next to him, locked in her frozen silence. What relation did she bear to the other? It was as though he had picked someone out of

124

a crowd, gone hurrying forward, only to realize, too late, his mistake, and that polite apologies were needed—"Excuse me, I thought you were someone I knew." He tried to remember what she had been like with her slim, almost boy's body twisting luxuriously under his, the great mass of her hair thick and coarse as a mane, and the colour—honey and late-afternoon sunlight—her voice calling to him, her smell, his fingers painful, as though she were fire and his fingers were moths, fluttering and fumbling in an ecstasy of warmth and self-destruction. She had been gentle, slowly roused, until suddenly her whole body would ignite and he would burn himself out with a great final shudder of joy. He knew he had loved her passionately in the true sense of the word—had *suffered*, willingly, lived for their meetings, neglected his painting, his parents, everything, until even she had cautioned him—"Don't make me your whole life. Save a part of yourself." Yet after she had gone, his canvases often remained blank or unfinished, his relations with his parents had, if anything, deteriorated. It was as though she had been his sun and he needed her to warm him, to smile down at him. And now this. An ice-maiden, the snow queen.

He remembered how in the old romances the beautiful maiden turns into a hag if the wrong questions are asked, if the right answers are not given. He stood now, defeated, horrified to discover that he hated her—not only for what she had become, but for what he had become: a false knight, an impostor.

"Do you really want to go through with this?" He started, hot with shame. But it was she who had spoken, still turned away, over her shoulder.

"No," he said miserably. "Do you?" Why not tell the truth? Why not finish it, be swift and sure and surely to God more honourable. His heart raced as he said the words.

She faced him. "No." Then, with a sigh, "Shall I tell you

something?" He waited. "When I wrote to you, I was frightened, ashamed, desperate, angry at you because you were so far away and I had to sit at home, running water in the bath so they wouldn't hear me being sick, letting my clothes out late at night when they were asleep, hoping my mother wouldn't wake up and come in to challenge me. I even thought for a while—No," she said, "never mind what I thought."

"You thought you'd get rid of it?"

"All right. I thought I'd get rid of it. And don't misunderstand me. It wasn't honour or pride or courage or anything of the sort that kept me from it. I was afraid, terrified. I thought I would die or be maimed in some way. But I didn't want the baby and I didn't want you—not like that, handcuffed."

"Yet you came back."

"I came back because I couldn't stand it at home."

"Don't you know what it's going to be like here?"

She looked at him sadly. "Terrible. But they will be strangers, don't you see? I hardly know them. Strangers can't hurt me, not really." She sighed.

"Yet on the plane I kept thinking maybe we'll crash or maybe I can get out of the gates before he sees me and lose myself in London, go to one of these homes or be an *au-pair* girl for a doctor's family—things like that. Look," she said and took off her hat.

"Oh God"—the tears ran down his face—"I didn't notice. Forgive me, I didn't notice."

"I did it last week. I couldn't stand it. It reminded me too much. . ." She paused.

"Were you hoping I wouldn't come?" She took his hands —four hands colder than ice, drowning people reaching out to each other for support, for strength, as the darkness closed over their heads.

126

"Worse." His turn to look away. His voice was thick, clotted. "Much worse."

"You were hoping I'd crash?"

"When they said the plane was delayed. . ." He stood silent, head bowed, holding desperately now to her hands.

Then, quite unexpectedly, she laughed—clear, happy laughter which shattered icy walls, blew away the rain, defied the universe.

"I thought you would hate me if you knew."

"I did. I don't." The warmth of her laughter flowed over him, eased his tiredness. He stood erect.

"Have you been standing here thinking horrible thoughts about me?"

"Terrible." She laughed again. "How terrible you'll never know."

"About toothbrushes?"

"Worse." He too began to laugh, felt the laughter boil up in him from some hidden place.

"Worse," he shouted, "far worse!" They rocked together in the narrow corridor, hands linked to steady themselves against their swaying universe.

"Tell me," she begged.

"Never."

"Tell me."

He looked down at her wet face.

"Some day," he promised. "Some day I'll tell you everything."

When they returned to the compartment the train was slowing down again, and the grey-faced woman had already bundled up the baby in a worn shawl. They began to get their belongings together.

"That's all right then," said the traveller, stubbing out his cigar in the overflowing ashtray. Then he turned and gave the woman a ludicrous and lovely wink. The four of them moved down the corridor and the traveller began to hum as he thought of his wife and the dinner he knew was waiting.

"Remember?" whispered the girl, as they rocked against the swaying train. The boy smiled at her in the darkness.

"No rings. No elephants. Nothing. Does it matter?"

"Of course. But not much, now that we're here." The train pulled impatiently into the station.

AUNT HETTIE & THE GATES OF THE NEW JERUSALEM

Armed with a briefcase showing ominous bulges Aunt Hettie James waddles into view. I had a toy penguin once that walked like that—but only down an incline. Waddle, hesitate, other foot; waddle, hesitate. I see her from the upstairs window and turn back to my dressing table for another layer of lipstick. I'd rather be scolded for sins of commission than otherwise. Anyway, if you can control the area of attack you're better off. Still, what a pitiful figure—if she weren't such a bitch. Only God could have chosen her to be his agent—nobody else would have had the nerve.

I run down the stairs and catch her just as she's about to let herself in.

"Hello, Aunt Hettie. Hot, isn't it?" She wipes her face with a man's cotton bandanna. One of Grandpa's. She's been going through his drawers again.

"Hello, my dear. Are you alone?" (If I'd been alone I would have run and hid.)

"No ma'am. Mother's in the back yard. You can go through the house if you like." This to her retreating back. She needs no offers. Nosy, she examines everything through her pudgy eyelids. Up. Down. Sees the vacuum cleaner left lying out, the dust on a coffee table. Stops midway through the dining-room.

"Tell your mother a picture like that should always hang

at eye level." Continues through the kitchen. "Clara. . . Clare-AH!" Sometimes I wish I were dead. No, I don't, I wish she were dead. "Tell your mother. . . ." But no rise to my bait. She must be after something bigger, more important. What does she carry in that briefcase, anyway, souls? Wherever she goes she leaves behind a stink of Listerine and self-righteousness. My aunt is afraid of nothing. . . except germs. I'd like to find a really nice typhoid case. I'd get Aunt Hettie over there on the excuse the poor soul wanted to be saved.

"Fuck," I say, trying it out. "Fuck fuck fuck and balls." (But not aloud.)

Voices in the back yard. My mother is cutting her some flowers. Aunt Hettie pulls out something that is probably chicken soup. My aunt's soups are almost as terrible as my aunt herself. I can't understand why Mother doesn't pour them down the drain. Maybe Aunt Hettie tells her they've been consecrated or something. Chicken soup in the briefcase—in a screw-top jar. Always practical. Doesn't want hot soup all over those souls. And tonight, undaunted by making chicken soup, or beds, or all those other "chores" she's always moaning about, she'll preach at the City Mission. She's the only woman I've ever met who still talks about "chores" instead of housework. I get a picture of woodpiles and hog butchering and rows of jewel-like preserves all neatly labelled. Ha. And she'll preach tonight. Sister Helen James. At the City Mission. Tonight. I saw it in the paper. At least she's my *mother's* sister.

My Aunt Hettie James lost her sense of taste when she lost her sense of smell. (Scarlet fever when she was very little. Or so she says.) But I observe her at Thanksgiving and Christmas.

"Turkey and ham and. . . sausages!" (Casts her eyes upward as if to say, "You see what I have to contend with!")

"Very nice I'm sure," she says in her very-nice-I-don't-think tone of voice. But manages to pass her plate for more. My grandfather smiles at me and raises his drumstick. She keeps house for him, walks around him saying, "When you're gone...," touches things as though *she* owned them. And reads the Bible to him every night. Thank God, he's deaf. Never the interesting bits. Once, when I stayed overnight, I asked to read instead. She nearly dropped her teeth with joy. "What shall we do with our little sister who has no breasts?" I made sure he heard that time, all right. We grinned at each other. (People say we even look alike.)

"It's right in there," I said. She wasn't amused. But that's not surprising. Nothing amuses her except making others as uncomfortable as possible. Sat on my bed, once, and asked:

"What would you do if Jesus came in and sat down beside you?" She couldn't understand why I thought this was so funny. I mean, out of the blue! But it would make quite a bedful: Aunt Hettie James and Jesus and myself. What would you do? What would she do, I wonder.

Speaking of breasts, I envy Aunt Hettie her breasts. What a waste on an aging virgin. Overripe, pear-shaped, really alive-looking. And to be hidden away in black serge and flannel. I have no shape. At thirteen I have given up hope. I do desperate exercises every morning. I must—I must—I must-increase-my-bust. And there it all is, on her. If I thought for one minute that's what religion can do. . . . But was she ever really human, I wonder. Did anyone ever want to fondle those? I doubt it. "Thou still unravished bride of quietness." We had to learn that for school, and somebody asked what "ravished" meant. Everybody else giggled. Still, she's not quiet. She even has a kind of religious snore when she's asleep. And awake, always talking, talking, talking. My brother said she has verbal diarrhea. I get a different picture—David and his pebbles, her words going ping, ping,

ping at anybody unfortunate enough to come within strik-
ing distance. Told me once to go into church work—meant
I was plain. I'd rather go to hell in my own way, and believe
me, I have plans. My mother says I ask for it, and I guess I
do. I like to annoy my aunt and watch her choose her pebbles.

"What have you got on your cheeks?"

"Nothing."

"Don't tell lies to your aunt, my dear. What have you got
on your cheeks?"

"Nothing. I rubbed them with a peach." She has to think
about this one. Peaches come from ABOVE. Finally:

"Just because you're a little sallow is no reason to tamper
with what God gave you." I'm tempted to show her my
padded bra, but even Mother doesn't know about that.

What does she dream about, when she snores so peacefully, this aunt of mine with the enormous boobs? Or maybe
people who are saved don't dream. She probably has visions
instead. But what does she see when she's naked and stands
before the mirror? Does she avert her eyes? She bathes
Grandpa in his underwear, he told me. Then leaves him to
take it off and towel himself. I think that's disgusting, but
maybe she thinks he is. I don't know much about bodies yet.
I've never seen a man naked, just my brother (until he got
so prudish) and once my father in the bathroom. He swore,
then said, "I'm sorry, please get out." It's like a sausage,
maybe. But really like nothing I'd ever seen before. And
what about my grandpa? When you get old, really old, what
happens to it? Is it like a woman? Does your hair turn white,
the thing itself shrivel up? What's she afraid of, anyway?
(But I don't dare tell my mother what my grandpa said.
Another row. And he wanted to live alone.)

My Aunt Hettie James is the skeleton in our closet. Or
would be, if she weren't so fat. Comes into our house with-

out knocking, causes trouble. Says we're not Christian, whatever that means; but seems to think something can be done
about me. (Probably because I'm female. I've certainly
never given her any encouragement in that direction.) If my
mother wants to get me mad, all she has to do is say, "Wipe
that smile off your face; you look just like your Aunt Hettie." Which is simply not true. I resemble Grandpa, nobody
else. Anyway, she'd be awfully funny if she were somebody
else's aunt. She's shaken with the Shakers, quaked with the
Quakers, rolled with the Rollers—everything. God she
really likes—but Man? Always has a row (usually about
how the collection money is spent) and leaves under a
cloud. Now she's independent (I think) and preaches at the
Mission once a week. After she's given Grandpa his bath
and seen he's tucked in bed. They put her picture in the paper—or she does. Must have been taken thirty years ago,
before she ran to fat. Marcelled hair, but the same smirky
smile. Sister Helen James. And sometimes kids at school
say, "Is that your aunt?" I'd fight them if I were only a boy.
But once my friend and I—I said we were going to the
movies—went down to the East Side to see her at the Mission. Boy, were we scared. It was awfully dark, and the
streets smelt of garlic and cabbages. Things like that. The
hall was shabby, too, with benches like bleachers at the foot-
ball stadium. There wasn't much light and there were maybe ten or a dozen people up near the front, all men. Drunks
and vagrants, I guess, who were glad to get in off the street.
(Mind you, she won't have anything to do with places like
the Salvation Army. Says it encourages them to be idle.)
She was up there in her black serge with a waxy-faced, pim-
ply man I'd never seen before. Called him Brother Harris.
He was playing the piano and she was singing that thing she
always sings in Grandpa's house. "Oh there's a joy—joy—
joy—joy—deep in my heart—deep in my heart (breath) to

stay." (Smirk.) Every time she breathed in she looked like Jayne Mansfield. In the bust, I mean. "You tell 'em, lady," said a dirty, faded-looking man in a cloth cap. And she just smiled her terrible "that's-all-right-sinner" smile and began her speech. I couldn't take it. It wasn't even funny any more. We snuck out. (Thank God she never saw us.)

Now she comes back with my mother. They're arguing—as usual. Or my mother is. Aunt Hettie never argues, she just makes superior faces.

"But that's where he belongs, and that's where he has to go. I really can... not... *cope*."

"Surely he can afford a private nurse?"

"You were always impractical." (Smirk.) "A private nurse is out of the question. Besides, he wouldn't want one in the house. He'll have to go to the Home."

My mother starts to cry, and my stomach goes all funny, like it always does when she cries.

"If it's a question of money—"

"Of course it's a question of money. Or partly. But you are hardly in a position to help out." (We're always broke, she knows it.)

"You've sponged off him ever since you came back. Now you just can't be bothered."

"Now just a minute." Aunt Hettie's voice goes sharp and hard, like pebbles. "I've looked after him for ten years. I've sacrificed my own wishes for his, laid aside my life's plan, everything but my one night a week at the Mission. With no reward except the knowledge that I've been a good daughter to him."

"With free room and board for ten years and everything your own way, you mean."

"Say what you like, if it makes you feel better. I know the truth and so does God. You can't hurt me. But the truth is, and you know it, he's senile and needs proper professional

134

care. I'm not a nurse, although" (smirk) "I certainly feel I've had enough experience in that line."

"He wants to die at home. It's his home, not yours."

Almost casually. "It will be mine when he's gone. But that has nothing to do with it. I can't afford a trained nurse, nor can you, and he needs one."

I'm terrified, want to shout at them, "Shut up, don't talk about him like that." To shout, "Grandpa, Grandpa, I'll look after you. I love you. Don't grow old. Don't let them take you away." They never look in my direction.

"You're nothing but a queer, twisted bitch." (My mother.)

"You're just emotionally upset." (My aunt.) "I've seen the doctor."

"What, one of your shyster doctors?"

"His own. Now don't be foolish. There are some forms we should both fill out."

My mother, weeping in great tearing sounds, rushes to the phone. My aunt makes her usual exit, having destroyed us all. At the door, she turns to me, huddled in the corner.

"Tell your mother I said thank you for the roses."

They sent him to the Home. Even my mother, in the end, agreed. I went every Sunday to see him. I'll swear he wasn't senile until they put him in. Now he sits in his dressing gown and shuts his eyes against unfamiliar walls and windows. He has shrunk, and gazes at me, his favourite, with dull blue eyes.

"Is that you, Clare?" (My grandma, he means.)

"No, Grandpa, it's me."

He remembers and tries to smile.

"Still chasing the boys?"

"You'd better believe it. Look, I brought you some magazines. *True Detective*, your favourite."

"Thank you." They lie in his lap and he doesn't even try

to turn the pages. "But don't spend your money on me. Here." He fumbles in his dressing gown pocket. It's a nice dressing gown, with blue brocaded trimming. I used to love it when I was smaller. He called it his "smoking jacket," because that used to make me laugh. He gives me a dollar, looking around defiantly first, hoping, maybe, that somebody will see.

"They can't take it all away, not till I'm dead. And then I wouldn't want it, would I?"

Even at thirteen I already know when you mustn't cry, and when you must receive.

"Thank you, Grandpa, I'll buy a new lipstick."

"That's right, don't let them get you down."

"Goodbye, Grandpa."

"Goodbye, Clare."

They always let me stay an extra ten minutes after they've visited with him. There are so many things I want to ask and tell him. But I guess I don't know the words yet. Anyway, at least I know he gets a proper bath and doesn't have to listen to the Bible every night.

For two years he stayed at the Home, but Aunt Hettie James never stopped coming to see us. My mother treated her very coolly, but since she had agreed, I couldn't see she had much justification for bitterness. I found it very hard to get back to the old relationship with my mother. We could probably have taken another loan. Or stopped her, somehow. But maybe you can't stop people like Aunt Hettie. Maybe that's what God is all about. If you believe in him— I don't. My mother keeps saying we should feel sorry for my aunt. I feel sorry for Grandpa. The walls in his room are the same colour as the halls at school. And we bring him flowers from the garden, which somehow only makes it worse.

Aunt Hettie James has taught herself to drive the old Packard, and managed to get a license. This makes her fatter than ever, but she can get to the Mission quicker (she goes every day now). And to our house. She's turned the upstairs of Grandpa's house into apartments. I wonder how the tenants feel about her. But maybe she leaves them alone. Cash seems as important as converts. Or maybe they have to be converted before she lets them in. Grandpa agreed. I don't think he really cared. She says it gives him an extra bit of income. To do what? She even bought me a Bible with my name on it this Christmas. I wanted to shove it down the toilet, but didn't dare. I've never opened it, and never even dust it. I hated her now, in earnest, and didn't even try to irritate her any more. I run away, usually, if I see her first.

He grew smaller every time I went to see him. And even his eyes, which I loved, got a paler and paler blue. His hands were very thin, and all the veins stood out.

"Is that you, Clare?"

"No, it's me."

And sometimes, trying desperately:

"Grandpa, do you remember when we used to go to Ross Park Zoo? Just you and me? You always bought some candy for the deer. Peppermint drops from that place on Seymour Street. Red and white. And an extra bag for us."

He laughed.

"We've had some good times, you and I." I have to say it.

"Grandpa, don't go." It's almost as though he walks away while I stand talking. "Look, I've brought you some magazines. *True Detective*, your favourite."

I never spend the dollars. I have them still.

Aunt Hettie holds me cruelly by the shoulders.

"Schoolwork on a Sunday?" (Smirk.) "Let me tell you a little story. When I was at college another student, a boy, and I were tied for first place all the final year. He was very, very bright, like you. And your poor old aunt had to work like the dickens to keep up with him. He used to study on a Sunday, too. I never studied on the Lord's Day, and prayed and read my Bible instead. I got first place, and always think there was a lesson in it. I'm sure it was a sign." Her fat, ringless hands dig into my flesh. (Iron underneath all that blubber. I want to ask, "And whatever became of him?") Her incredible breasts heave with the joy of past victories, as she breathes Listerine and holiness into my downcast face. I feel sick, and wish she'd take her hands off me.

"I pray about you. Oh, yes, I pray about you!" says my aunt. "Your aunt prays long and hard about you and your brother. If only your mother and father were good Christians."

My brother finds me crying.

"Don't let the old bitch bother you so much."

"I hate her."

He shrugs, interested in other things. A tennis racquet over one arm.

"Listen," I say, "are you coming with us Sunday?"

"To see Grandpa? Hell, I'd like to. I really wish I could."

"You didn't go last week."

"Well, I'll go next week, I promise."

"Get out," I scream at him. "Get your rotten self out of my room."

He shrugs and shuts the door as he goes out. Comes back in:

"Don't get Mother started, that's all I ask. You know what that's like, don't you?"

Where can you turn when you're not quite fifteen and you've got rotten parents and a rotten brother and a bitch for an aunt? Why grow up? All it means is to grow away. Selfish pigs, that's what we turn into. I wanted my grandpa back, to take me to the zoo and buy me candy. Peppermint drops, the red and white ones.

138

Aunt Hettie James is dreaming now of a mission of her own. She has us down to dinner (she's a terrible cook these days) and tells us of her plans. She found some rusted wrought iron gates at a junk yard and has painted them white. She keeps them in the spare garage, behind one of her tenants' cars. All wrapped up in plastic so they won't get dirty. She carefully removes the wraps and shows them off.

"One day," she says, "I'll use these for my mission."

"Where are you going to build it?" I ask, while the others stand there looking embarrassed.

"Build it?" She gestures toward the house. "Why should I have to build it? The Good Lord has given me a perfectly good place right here."

"Here?" Even my brother looks shocked. "In his house?"

"Oh, after he's gone, of course. I know my place." I want to claw that smirking face, to kick the gates, do something terrible.

"You wouldn't dare." My mother.

"My dear Clare, it is not a question of daring. It's my house when he's gone."

I see the sitting-room full of drunks. "You tell 'em, lady." Aunt Hettie at my grandmother's piano. The waxy, pimpled man, Brother Harris, sitting in my grandpa's favourite chair.

"He'll live to be a hundred. Then you'll see."

"She's like you, Clare, much too emotional. Her attitude to Father isn't healthy. And her manners are not all they should be, either." She stands there, a fat black spider, with her hand on one of the gates. Yet Grandpa would have liked them—as gates, I mean. They're full of tiny vines and little woven places.

Mother: "Have you told him?"

"Of course I've told him. Although I didn't have to." I know she's lying. So do we all. She stands there smirking.

"Listen," I say to Grandpa. "Do you know she wants to

139

build a mission—Aunt Hettie?"

He doesn't open his eyes. I wonder if he's heard me. (And I am frightened of what he'll do or say if he has. I'm sorry now I said it.)

"Your aunt's a damn fool." I smile with triumph. He can fix her.

"But I won't stop her. Not yet, anyway. After I'm gone, we'll see."

"Don't talk like that. You're not going to die, I know it."

"And don't you be a damn fool, either. Of course I've got to die. I'm sick. . . and tired." He sighed. "I'm tired of all this foolishness."

The nurse comes in and says it's time. I'm tiring him. I go back to my parents in the car. My mother:

"Is something wrong?" Starts to open the door in alarm.

"It's all right, nothing's the matter with him. Except he's old and I get sad, sometimes." She relaxes.

"What do you talk about, you two?"

"Nothing much. About when I was little. But I do all the talking lately." I begin to cry again.

My mother's face gets wrinkled, but I don't care.

"He's my father, you know. You seem to forget that sometimes. You act as though you own him, with all your sulks and secrets. I suffer too, believe me. Maybe your aunt is right; it's not very healthy, your attitude toward Grandpa."

"Shut up. Shut up shut up shut up!" My father slaps me.

Aunt Hettie James phones us just before supper.

"He's going fast, you'd better hurry."

Suddenly I don't want anything to do with it. I think perhaps I could face it when he's dead, and final. But dying? I cry and say I've got a headache. Mother says I'm unnatural. My father says, "For Christ's sake, isn't it bad enough. . . ." My brother says, "And you were the one. . . ." I wash my face and go. Reluctantly.

140

Assembled, we all look down on him. I find I can't cry any more. I'm frightened. His eyes are closed and he is struggling to catch his breath. My mother weeps, my brother too, which really frightens me. I try to think of other places, other times. He's dead. The nurse goes out, with her professional face and stiff white skirts. My aunt begins to sing, eyes shut, breasts thrusting toward heaven. "Just—a—clos—er—walk—with—thee." Nobody stops her. I can't stand it.

"Are you satisfied now?" I demand. "Isn't this what you wanted?"

She opens her eyes, and I see only triumph shining there.

"I pity you, you have no faith, poor child." She starts to rock backward, forward, swinging her breasts from side to side. "Just—a—clos—er—walk—with—thee." My brother grabs me, pushes me out the door.

"Can't you behave for once?" And then I start to cry.

He left my mother money, and my brother money in a trust. He left my aunt the house, but only for her lifetime. Then it comes back to me. Triumphant, I go down to see her. Already she's taking pictures off the walls. I tell her she will build no mission here. She smirks and says, "We'll see," and starts to hum.

But I'll see first. I'll see her rot in hell before she ever hangs those gates in front of my house.

A WINTER'S TALE

Some memories are butterflies, swift, graceful, leaving behind a sense of summer and contented hovering. The delicate, fluttering ones. No harm in these. Some are cathedral windows, butterfly wings on a solemn scale. Crimson, emerald, sapphire. Jewelled truths. Cold, perhaps, because reflections only, but leaving behind a thrill and terror of organ music and the smell of grapes. Communion. Or memories like bats—unseen and only sensed in the dark and dusty corners of the night. No voice speaks, and nothing is heard but the silent, terrible scream of the sleeper, struggling to awake. Or luna moths, soft and veined like thighs. Night thoughts. Or wingless completely—maggots in rotting meat.

Which is this, then—or none—or all? You judge. I remember the snow which fell like a blessing on our shoulders. I remember his words—but not the sound of his voice. "Is it all right to call you darling in bed?" I remember the sleeping town, crumbling yet strong in its granite unconcern for the lovers it had seen before and would see again. I remember it all, as though it were today.

It is easier to conjure up a fairy tale (which is what I could do right now and write it down correctly, according to the rules) than to put one's finger on the pulse of truth. In the tale it is all so easy. I, the princess, and he, the prince. We meet and of a sudden fall in love. There are dragons, of course, and wicked dukes and many other dangers; but these can all be banished, crushed or conquered. We mount the milk-white steed, ride off into the silver dawn. No sequel; nothing sordid. When the storytellers say "The end" they mean it. Never the names of Cinderella's children. Yet he and I were once upon a time (but only once) like the prince and princess. He woke me with a kiss, freed me from chains of loneliness and dragons of despair—if only for an evening. For what he woke me to, and what he freed me from, I should, I suppose, be grateful.

One night, once upon a time. That's all. One silent winter's night it was, when the snow fell in great flakes until the whole sky seemed to be alive with wings—the ghosts of a million butterflies or moths.

It was, I suppose, on the morning after, when I woke early and remembered, "You're twenty-one and still a virgin!" that I opened the door (or at least unlocked it) to the events which were to follow. Not that I hadn't considered the fact before. But it was usually as a form of parlour game with other girls at college.

Someone would start—"I wonder how many of us are really virgins." And some would proudly boast that they were not (often the liars), while others would laugh uneasily and proudly boast they were. Still others would turn away and smile. Yet most of us agreed it wasn't worth it—degrading, somehow, to have no control; "Unless, of course," someone inevitably added, "you're really in love." But that's the trouble, isn't it? Songs, mothers, friends and guidance counsellors: everyone assured us we would know—and we believed them. The very young still dream of shining knights who will awaken them with kisses from their innocent, tormented dreams. And desperate, heavy-thighed with spring, they allow themselves to be awakened in a dark car or a deserted lane by someone who, in the long daylight of Later

143

On, which stretches before them like a northern winter, turns out to be neither a prince, nor charming. I hadn't allowed that to happen—avoided the cars and the lanes. I all but avoided the spring. I was not only prudent but afraid—afraid of the dark, masculine laughter and the promise of new delights. I prided myself on my fear and knew I was right.

But now I wanted nothing more, on this winter morning in this strange mediaeval town, than to be that which I had shunned before. I was cold in a new way—not cold by choice but rather (why hadn't I seen it?) cold by destiny. I lay wide-eyed and shivering in the wet dawn; my roommate, only the top of her pale hair showing from beneath the mound of blankets, was asleep. She slept the sleep of the uncomplicated —and the beautiful. If I ever were to write my fairy tale it is she who would be the princess. Beautiful and good and innocent. It is a truism, I suppose, that the pretty girl chooses the plain girl for her friend; but the reasons are not so simple, or so selfish, as one might think. Often the pretty needs the plain not as foil, but counterfoil—an official sign that there is more to her (the pretty one) than meets the eye. She was uncomplicated, yes, but passionate, forever in love—it seemed to be a necessary condition to her survival. Yet the passion would soon die down and she would move on to a new partner, still searching and still innocent, and still (this was something to marvel at) untarnished. Still a virgin. We had known each other more than two years and were the best of friends, although her reasons for virginity—a deep, religious repugnance to something she felt was so unsanctified and therefore sinful—were different from my own. She was not cold, but simply committed to a dream. And now I reflected that her chances of finding it, and of losing her virginity, were infinitely better than mine.

I was never beautiful—not even as a baby. But as a child

144

—and later—I believed that I would, of necessity, become so. Then, somewhere around my seventeenth year, I had realized, and accepted, that this was not to be, and I laid that dream aside, firmly but with regret, the way one might lay aside a favourite dress which has suddenly become too shabby or too small. I took refuge in the fact that I was not, at least, ugly and might even become, with time and perseverance, attractive. I also took refuge in my intelligence. And this was a great bond between us, my roommate and me. (For the good fairies of our childhood had, with her, left nothing out.) We could discuss things—not just men—together. Together we discovered the world of books: philosophy, history, fiction; and together thrilled to their voices: now angry, now sad, now gentle, now morose. We even felt, sometimes, we had grown up together (which perhaps we had) and could often read each other's thoughts, anticipate each other's reactions. A marital relationship if you like, but one which exists most often between two women or two men. That morning I was glad she was asleep when I woke up hearing that "still" so loudly in my ears. "Twenty-one and still a virgin." I was terribly conscious of my body, warm beneath the many layers of blanket, and for the first time conceived of my "maidenhead" (such a poetic term!) as something already drooping on the stem. Suddenly I wanted to be something else than "still a virgin," wanted to give myself, that was it, to give *myself*, that is to say my body, to someone else. It was no longer a question of avoiding being taken. I wanted to know it all—what it was like to hesitate and then succumb, what it was like to be roused to such a pitch of wanting that all scruples, reservations, built-in checks would be lost upon my body screaming to be touched and touched and taken. I wanted to know what it was like to fall asleep and waken to the pressure of another person in the bed. I wanted everything.

My precious intelligence said not to be so foolish, that the words which had been spoken so mockingly (and they had been spoken to me, not about me, flung down as a careless challenge I could pick up or ignore) should be received as they were given—lightly, as a jest. He had, after all, been tight. And so had I and so had everyone else.

I can see him still, leaning against the mantelpiece, observing the others (an after-play party and many still with their make-up on: Lonnie Donnegan filling the smoky air with his pulsing voice, the nervous, overexcited chatter which was a symptom of relief and relaxation; Macduff jiving with Lady Macbeth; the fat girl who had been prompted telling everyone how she lost the place at a crucial moment, demanding her share of attention and drinking too much and too quickly). I thought, "If the devil were to show himself on earth he would look like this man: intelligent, tall, lean, somehow sulphuric and dangerous." I knew who he was, of course (who didn't?), knew his girlfriend too, a shy dark-haired girl who wore no make-up, and yet was beautiful, as beautiful as my golden roommate—Rose-red to Snow-white. Knew also that they were lovers, although she did not live with him, but with three other girls in a flat not far from our boarding house; had seen them together at parties, she rarely speaking, he always, or usually, surrounded by a group of admirers, male and female. For he was brilliant, and when drunk would let forth a flow of words, of speculations and pronouncements which took one's breath away by their very simplicity and power. And although she was beautiful, many said (both male and female, particularly the hangers-on), "What does he see in her?" I had wondered myself, for he did not look the type who would seek out goodness, deliberately, unless it were to destroy it—certainly not to establish anything so permanent as the relationship which they so obviously had. Then one day I had seen them, sitting on a mound above the battlements of the ruined castle (the castle which had made the choice of the play so obvious, once someone had suggested it). It was late October and cool; but the sun was making a wan attempt to warm the earth, looking somehow sad, convalescent, in the blue-grey sky; and few had left their books or gas fires to come out and watch the rehearsals. They sat there, he leaning back on his elbows, his face tilted upward, eyes closed, somehow more arrogant than ever, while she read a book.

Suddenly he leaned over and whispered something to her. She got up, put her book down carefully, marking the page with a bit of paper. Then she gathered her scarlet gown around her and rolled, like a child, over and over, down the slope to the bottom. She ran back up, her pale face flushed with delight, and he took her in his arms and kissed her. Then she picked up her book and they walked away. I knew, then, what he saw in her, and why, although I kept silent (I had been an unknown witness after all) when the inevitable question was raised.

Yet this evening he was alone, without her, offered no explanations, simply came in late and took up his stand by the mantelpiece, leaving it only to get another drink from time to time. I too was alone, had hurried home to wash off the make-up (I was not enough of an exhibitionist to wish to appear as a witch at a small gathering with no audience-actor barrier to separate me from my friends and fellow-students). My roommate had come with her latest knight, a young doctor, and was very gay (and very beautiful) across the room.

That he and I should speak to each other was inevitable, for I was sitting on the floor directly below him, and, like him, observing. He looked down and then said:

"You were very good."

"It is hardly a part at which one could fail." I smiled up

at him, for he was interesting, if, from my point of view, unapproachable, and not only because he "belonged," if that is the right word, to someone else.

"You're wrong, you know. There are witches and witches. You made me feel that you were not evil, which is the standard interpretation, but inexorable. And," he added, somewhat inconsequentially, "I liked your hair." (They had silvered it for the part; but I had washed it before coming out—even at the risk of a cold. It reminded me of death, I suppose, though that might not have occurred to me then.)

"Well, I didn't. Perhaps for the play. A 'secret black and midnight hag' would look silly with red hair."

"You flatter yourself. Your hair is not red, it's brown." I was annoyed. Even a plain girl usually has one feature of which she is proud, or at least relies on to feed her feeble vanity. Mine was my hair.

"It's red."

He sat down, then, next to me, crossing his long legs tailor-fashion. "Perhaps I haven't really looked at it." Right then I felt as I would if a window had suddenly been opened directly behind my neck, that I would want to—wanted to—move away.

Then, "Are you a virgin?" Very low. In the smoke and dimness it was difficult to tell if he were smiling.

"Yes," I said, and stood up, searched frantically, looking for someone who could serve as an excuse for a graceful, if hurried, exit. No-one. I stood there, and he laughed, mocking me.

"How old are you?"

"Does it matter?" I was angry with him, with myself, with the dark-haired girl who should have been by his side.

"In your case I should think it does."

"I'm twenty-one."

"Twenty-one and still a virgin!" Then he laughed again,

148

got up abruptly and left the party, saying goodnight to no-one, walking through the crowd like a displaced god.

On the way home, alone and in spite of my damp hair, I wandered toward the ruined abbey, one of my favourite spots in a town so steeped in history and fable the very damp oozed mystery. On the left stood the battlements of the once forbidding castle—where we had played *Macbeth* that very night, in spite of the cold and the wet. Farther along and up, a cross, marking the death of their first student martyr, was built into the street. A small dog walks, they said, six feet above the pavements, ghosts making no allowance for sub-sidence. Wherever one turned one was met with Romance; but of it all I loved the abbey, and its nun, the best. Nothing was left but one broken wall and if you chose at midnight you could put your hand in through a grille and feel her ghostly fingers touching yours. They said she killed herself for love, was beautiful but true. A fable probably, but I went back that night to see if she could give me reassurance. I leaned my face against the rough stone and touched her hand. I was terribly troubled—too much excitement, little food and too much drink. I touched her hand (I think), but nothing happened. No sense of kinship, of principles glori-fied, only a sense of something dead and dull.

From there I wandered to the sea, which guards and threatens the old town. The moon was out, and through the mist I could see quite clearly the line between earth and water. But the night sound of the waves, in which I usually delighted, did nothing to calm me and I turned toward home. My roommate was asleep when I got in—asleep when I awoke. I caught a cold, which was to be expected.

When I was better and about again I heard the story of why he had been alone that night. (And all the time I lay in bed I wondered if he had asked about me. I felt it was his fault

I had a cold, his fault I was so restless, couldn't read, could barely carry on a conversation. And yet I wouldn't ask about him—couldn't.) He'd had a row, or so the story went. I was somehow relieved—his mockery was not, after all, directed at me alone. But such was his unique place amid our circle (the circle in which I was included not only because I was my roommate's roommate but because I was new and therefore "interesting") that no-one knew more than that. And when, a few days later, the two of them were seen walking together, as usual, there was nothing more said except (with varying degrees of jealousy or satisfaction depending upon the speaker), "They've made it up."

And so, although he had awakened something in me which would not now sleep, the something remained general—an undirected longing, a sense of myself as a cup (a family heirloom, perhaps? I mocked) waiting to be filled.

I went to dances (plain girls who are intelligent and brave make it a point of honour to be good dancers); parties (plain girls who are intelligent make it a point of honour to be witty without being coarse, to learn to drink without getting drunk—to be, if not "in demand," at least worth inviting); studied hard and had midnight discussions, over beef tea or coffee, with my roommate (I was beginning to wonder if the young doctor were not, perhaps, her knight after all) and with my fellow boarders. We solved questions of life, religion, politics one night, only to destroy the solutions, as a child will destroy the sand castle he has built, the next. In other words I participated and was content—at least until the final goodnights were said, my roommate was asleep and I was left alone with my twenty-one years—and my virginity. I dreamt, but my hero, when there was one, remained faceless or out of focus, simply The Hero, perhaps the old god Thor. Naturally I saw *him* at parties, public lectures, dances, in the tea rooms, on the street. Saw him and her I should say, for they were one in my mind. They were a relationship rather than two separate individuals. I made sure I never got too close, although I did not think he would repeat his words, realized (in my intelligent part at least) that he had probably forgotten them. Our eyes never met, although we said the usual "hellos," made the necessary social gesture of formal recognition when the occasion called for it.

And so it might have gone on, and there would have been no memories and no story, if it had not been for one fact, one circumstance which blew away my safety, my carefully constructed castle, as surely as if a cannon had been fired point-blank. For, as well as being plain, I was poor. One thinks of Americans in Europe as being at least reasonably well-to-do, but this is not always the case. I was not unique, for there were, and are, many others like me, who through their own efforts—or those of their parents—have begged, borrowed, worked summers, evenings, done God knows what to follow the still-fresh American dream of Europe as a Mecca of culture and tradition. Wasn't that part of the charm of this particular place? The scarlet gowns, the ruined castle, the abbey, the local ghosts, the grey buildings which had a patina of history, like old silver, on their stony sides? Romance—that is what we lack in America and what we seek among the spires of Oxford, the studios of Paris, or in my case the cobbled streets of a Scottish university town. We call it "education," or "broadening one's outlook," but its real name is Romance. Yet if one is poor, and one manages to get there at all, one has to, at some point, compromise. My compromise was painless but necessary: I would not travel during the Christmas "vac," and then, in the spring, my roommate and I would go south, to Spain, for two weeks. She was going skiing at Christmas with some of the people from the boarding house (regretting already her departure, however temporary, from the young doctor, but at the same time anticipating Austria—and another chance to travel). She did not offer to lend me money, for she knew, without being told, that our relationship would never be the same if she did, even if I refused (which she knew I would). And I could have gone somewhere—had invitations to London, to a friend in Dundee, to people from the boarding house itself, who were "going down" for Christmas. I did not refuse out of a sense of martyrdom; but the idea of Christmas with a family other than my own (and, even with my own, Christmas was always something of a strain—a too-hectic renewal of outgrown relationships, festivity as flushed as fever, overeating, too many questions and I with inadequate answers) distressed me. I said I had work to do (which was true) and, in a way, was relieved when they all left and I could be alone. I went out of the station, and turned, not toward the way home, but down to the beach, walking aimlessly—no thoughts, just a sense of freedom and an awareness of sound—the damp sand's suck-suck at my shoes, the great inhale-exhale of the sea, the "mee-mee-mee" of the gulls, like spoiled children fighting over toys. I found a bit of stick, wet, washed up by the sea, and dragged it behind me as though I had a companion who walked on one incredibly pointed leg. Then I stopped and drew a figure in the sand, again aimlessly, hardly aware of what I was doing, a stick figure, neither male nor female, simply a sign (to whom? the sand? the great North Sea?) that someone had been there. I stood and watched the waves run up to it and then, afraid, run back again on their silver feet, up, back, up, back, finally touching it, then pouncing on it quietly, quickly, giving it little cat-licks, until it disappeared. It was only then that I felt lost rather than alone, and I hurried back toward the town and the security of the boarding house.

That evening, I took a hand mirror (the only one there

was, unless I went down the hall to the bathroom) and examined myself, naked and shivering in spite of the gas fire
which hummed merrily at the end of the room. I could see
my toes and a bit of my calves, then part of my legs and my
knees. And so on up to my face, my plain, sensible, intelligent face. Yet of course one could not be objective. The me
I saw, or the fragments of me which I could summon with
a flick of my wrist downward or upward, had no external
reality. I wondered what I would look like to someone else,
standing naked, flat-bellied, straight-legged on the worn
carpet. I tried to imagine myself pregnant, my flat stomach
swollen with importance, sharing its secret with anyone who
cared to stop and look. When I was a child and exchanged
scraps of knowledge (overheard, misinterpreted, mangled
by ignorance and innocence) with other children, I had received with delight the information that babies came out of
your bellybutton. It was an exciting idea, and a pleasant one.
I would swell and swell until one day, "pop"—my child
would fly out like a genie summoned from a bottle. When
I told my older sister (for the knowledge and wonder, the
beautiful simplicity of the thing, needed to be told to someone else) she laughed and gave me the correct—and to me,
infinitely less romantic—version. I did not attempt to argue,
did not doubt that what she told me was true; for I was
learning that the nasty explanations in life were usually the
true ones. Yet I felt cheated somehow, and ashamed, and
kept the terrible secret, for once, to myself. I looked back
on that child now with a certain amount of awe. For even
after what my sister had told me I had never doubted that
some day I would have a baby, just as some day I would be
beautiful and married. "Twenty-one and still a virgin!" I
said to myself as I turned off the gas and prepared for sleep
in my neat and narrow bed.

Several newcomers had arrived at the boarding house when the halls closed for Christmas—bits of flotsam and jetsam, thrown up like myself by the tide of the great public holiday.

The African next door, lips protruding from his face as though they had been added later, after the head had been modelled, as a child adds features to a head made of clay or plasticine. He had brought a portable phonograph which he played at night (I knew, for once I knelt down and peeked under his door), in the dark, while he was asleep or lying down. French lessons, lessons in British history, and once the great bell-boom of Dylan Thomas, *A Child's Christmas in Wales*. I was intrigued by the African, but he never answered my greetings with more than a swift and soon-extinguished smile, a smile like a skilled arpeggio upon a keyboard. Someone had probably told him to smile at all the Whites before he left the tropics, poor thing. He ate his meals out and once I was disloyal enough to wonder if he ate with his fingers; and once I wondered, but only casually, scientifically you might say, what it would be like to knock on his door one night and walk in naked, walk over to his bed in the dark and turn the records off. I had a feeling he might scream, for he looked very serious. There was a French girl, whom I already knew by sight, studying for some external degree, teaching primary school and hating it. She descended to the dining-room every morning, always cold and discontented, with great red chilblained hands. She ate quickly, muttering to herself, devouring sausages the way she devoured knowledge. The landlady had asked me to be nice to her, and I had invited her to my room one night for a drink; she had poured out her hatred of the place, her homesickness for France, her need to distinguish herself. And, although I had listened sympathetically, or tried to, her ugly, square figure, her sullen face, her general atmosphere of dissatisfaction made me uneasy. She was older than I and reputedly very brilliant, and I could not help seeing certain parallels, however tenuous—myself in a boarding house ten years hence, chattering away about a thesis to someone, anyone who would listen and pretend to admire.

One other room had been let to a young Indian medical student, who uncoiled himself for breakfast, lunch and tea, then coiled himself up again to the thick books on anatomy, physiology, God-knows-what, lined up precisely on his mantelpiece. He had a slightly out-of-focus picture of his wife and child back in India, which he showed me once, in a rare moment of friendliness. I admired it, of course, although to me it was just an exotic blur. He said the picture helped him to study better, then whispered a polite, "If you will excuse me," and went down the hall to his room.

They were all so serious, so dedicated; I the hypocrite among them, carefully displaying my books for the day on my little table, leaving my door open so that they could see, if they stopped to look, how busy, how equally serious, *I* was; and putting the same books away, unread or unremembered, each night when I closed the door. Except for my sex I was not unlike the drone—a drone among the workers— yet my humming gas fire and my bent, studious back gave the illusion that I was what I was not. My restlessness, after the first few days, drove me back again and again to the sea, where at least I felt unashamed of my idleness, too insignificant to be regarded as anything—much less an idler. It was when I returned from one of these expeditions, these purgings of guilt for not making good use of my time, that I discovered him in my room, leaning against the mantelpiece, just as he had leaned that night. He saw me in the doorway and said peremptorily:

"Have you got a shilling? The fire's gone out." I went to the bedside table and opened the cigarette tin in which we kept the shillings for the meter. I handed him one and he stooped down, quickly lighting the fire, and said over his shoulder, "There's a trick to these, you know. I used to use the same shilling over and over in one place I lived."

"It would have shown up on the meter."

He stood up. "There's a trick to that too, a more elaborate one. It involves the landlady or," (he smiled) "her daughter." I stood there in my coat, wondering why he had come, what he wanted from me.

"Aren't you going to ask me in?"

"You are in."

"Only technically—I can see that by your face."

"Please sit down. I'm sorry, I'm just surprised to see you."

"You mean surprised that I'm still in town or surprised to see me here?"

"Both."

"I've been to Edinburgh for a few days, but I had work to do, so I'm staying here over the vac."

"Of course. You take your degree this year."

"Take it with honours, I hope." He stretched his long legs out to the fire, and leaned back in our one and only easy chair. It seemed only natural to offer him a cup of tea, to methodically hang up my coat, take the electric kettle to the bathroom and fill it, come back and plug it in, sit across from him (but on the floor) waiting for it to boil. He had closed his eyes and I was shocked to see how tired he looked —shocked and gratified; it made him, somehow, more human. When the kettle boiled I found two mugs, a tin of milk, sugar and a packet of biscuits. I thought he had fallen asleep, he was so still; so I sat there helplessly (but not discontented) with the biscuits on the floor between us.

He opened his eyes. "Milk, please, and no sugar." I held out the mug to him and he acknowledged my hospitality with another of his strange smiles (they could hardly be called "grins," yet I had the feeling that that was what they

156

were, that he was mocking me).

"Are you always prepared for any emergency?"

"What do you mean?"

"The type who always has a shilling for the meter, a kettle that works, milk, sugar, biscuits—the lot."

"I would like to be."

"You wouldn't find it boring?"

"How could it be boring? One would be so busy trying to anticipate all the emergencies, in order to prepare for them, one wouldn't have time to be bored."

"And if one found, in the end, that one had shelves and shelves of useless stuff—that one had never encountered any of the emergencies for which one had prepared...?"

"You're mocking me."

"Not at all. I'm just pointing out to you the deadliness of such a philosophy." He reached over and helped himself to another biscuit. I noticed his nails were bitten, and relaxed.

"Suppose I were to ask you out tonight, would you be prepared for that?" I realized, then, that this was exactly what I had been anticipating, preparing for, since I first entered the room—and perhaps before?

"I couldn't go."

"Couldn't because you can't or couldn't because you won't?"

"Does it matter?"

"Yes, as a matter of fact it does." And a look passed between us as silent and swift as stolen money exchanging hands.

"Because I am, as you would probably put it, 'taken'?"

"It would be dishonest."

"That depends on your definition of honesty. If I tell you honestly that I am bored and restless and lonely, and that I want to spend the evening with you, who are also bored and restless and lonely, is that dishonest?"

"To tell me, no. For me to take you up on it—yes."

"So you would rather stay here and pretend to read all these attractively arranged tomes," (he gestured toward the little table) "than come out with me."

"I didn't say I would rather; I simply said I wouldn't go out with you."

It had grown dark and I stood up, surprised to find that I ached with tension. I had thought I was managing so well! Everything seemed a bit far away, as though I were coming down with flu. When I switched on the light he closed his eyes. "Don't." I switched it off again.

"Tell me," he said, "do you believe in God?"

"Is it important?"

"Possibly."

I went to the window and stared out, other windows casting little paving stones of light along the dark street.

"I like to believe there was a God."

"What happened to him then?"

"He made the world—and then he died." (A cat and a mouse, casual, playing with words in order to retreat, advance. If we could keep on talking!)

He laughed, "Of what? Of overwork?"

"Of loneliness. You see, it was very beautiful, but imperfect—like all beautiful things. He couldn't, being perfect himself, being perfection rather—get down."

"Down to earth?"

"Exactly."

"And so he died?"

"Wouldn't you?" (I turned and watched the fire. Little, cold, blue fingers playing on the flame.)

"And what did this curious God of yours ever do for you?"

"I told you. He made the world."

"And that's enough?"

"That's all there is."

"Come here," he said, and when I sat down beside him he opened his eyes and looked down at me.

"If God is dead, and you are grateful to him, then why are you afraid?"

"Of him?"

"Of him—and me."

"You see a connection then?" I was too tired to refute him.

"I think I see. You wish that you could wait for some perfection—one moment, at least, to offer him, to make up to him for what he lost."

"I'll disappoint myself if I do not."

"You love me?"

"No." (Not love, no—what burned in that room was not love.)

"You know I don't love you?"

"Yes." We were not playing now. I shivered.

"And you think that things—worlds—situations such as what could occur tonight—should be created out of love?"

I struggled valiantly (I thought then) to return to the game. "I never said he created the world out of love."

"But that's what you meant."

"Not exactly. I don't know why he did it. I've often wondered. Bored perhaps—or lonely."

"But I am bored and lonely—and so are you. Can't we create a world? Wasn't the whole trouble that there was no-one to share his loneliness?" Heaps of words, pebbles collected on deserted beaches. Arrange them in curious designs. Use them for windows and doors, for stately paths and promenades. If one is interested in the moment, what does it matter that the tide is coming in or that a small child runs along the beach and kicks the castle in? We stood up together and I got my coat.

"Don't be afraid," he said, and I closed the door quietly.

We went down the stairs, moving against the accusing silence of the shut doors of my studious, serious neighbours.

"Where are we going?"

"To my flat."

It was nearly dawn when we returned, and the snow muffled our footsteps as though it, too, were a conspirator. At the corner, under the streetlamp, where the great white flakes, like moths, hurled themselves against the light, he kissed me, lightly, and was gone.

"No regrets," he had said and, "No regrets," I had achingly replied. Then I turned and walked slowly toward the house. I never saw him—alone—again.

SALON DES REFUSES

Toot-toot woke suddenly, jerked upright as though she had been pulled by an invisible string. The pale sunlight of a winter dawn, cold as a false smile, sidled through the bars and deposited small parcels of light on the floor. Toot-toot lay down again, stuck her head over the edge of the bed and watched the little squares of light. She reached out her pudgy hands and tried to coax the sunlight to her, wanted one of the little boxes to open and to play with under the thin blanket. "Toot-toot," she whispered softly, "toot-toot." Her pigtails stuck straight out from her head, as in a child's drawing. She reached too far and fell off the bed in a tangle of blanket and sheet. Snow thudding from the steep roofs in a winter thaw. Toot-toot did not care; her hands had reached a square of light. She lay happily, fondling the light, a royal child playing with building blocks of gold. "Toot-toot," she crowed happily from her tangled nest, a small cockerel greeting the false dawn. Eleanor La Douce, her black eyes shooting around the room like hot coals and coming to rest on the small figure playing on the floor, jumped out of bed and snatched the blocks of sunlight, ran screeching around the room. "You're a whore," she shrieked at Toot-toot. "You're a whore like all the rest of them. Fiends fiends fiends," she muttered, staring at her empty hands. "They have stolen from me my diamond brooch, my string of pearls, my son, my château on the Loire. Has it come to this, that the wife of General La Douce should be forced to steal from such as you?" Her skinny arm snaked out and slashed the air with a sound like wind in broken branches. Toot-toot cried quietly upon the floor. "Fuck you," said Eleanor La Douce.

Mother Brown heaved herself up the hill from the bus stop, the wind stinging her eyes, darting obscenely under last year's coat, playing tunes with icy fingers up and down her fat thighs, blowing down her neck with a rude kiss, howling away like a whole mob of naughty schoolboys. If the storm kept up tomorrow she would have to take a taxi. She thought resentfully of the taxi fare, of spending money. Wops and kikes, all of them, take the longest way round and fill their pockets with her hard-earned cash. Her resentment warmed her and she made it up the rest of the hill and across the compound without difficulty. Perhaps she could claim for taxi fare, being a widow and all that, and the varicose veins. It wasn't as if they had people standing in line to work there. Still, she'd have to go carefully—fifty a week was nothing to sneeze at. She thought of her account at the First City, swelling slowly and methodically like a woman great with child. And she thought of the brochures on Florida and California. Her anger melted like snow in sunlight and she was smiling happily as she waddled through the glass doors, pausing to stamp her feet and polish her bifocals, which had misted up in the sudden warmth of the building.

"Well, Mrs. Brown," said the gold-rimmed Director as he signed her in, "you look like the cat that swallowed the canary." On the wall behind the desk was a huge map of the compound and, in the corner, a globe. The desk was a jumble of papers, with pink and yellow memos stuck, like pastel butterflies, on spindles. She was about to tell him about the long walk from the bus stop, but two policemen came in the office, a grey little man swaying between them, so she went out, her galoshes making a suck-suck sound as she padded across the hall and turned the key which would bring the elevator down. She was early and there was no-one else waiting. A huge aluminum Christmas tree preened itself in the centre of the hall and the janitor had already turned on the light wheel underneath. The grey metal branches turned pale and pretty shades of blue, red, yellow, green. Very nice and of course they couldn't take a chance on fire, but she preferred the real thing herself; bet it cost plenty though. She thought of the taxi again and frowned. Throwing their money away on foolishness. State-controlled, of course. Always plenty of graft in a state-controlled institution. Still—fifty a week. She patted her black plastic handbag. She'd have to nip up and see when Cynthia was off for lunch. She wondered what she'd think of the brochures. Of course if two went in together on a thing like this it would be even cheaper. Still, Cynthia was a Catholic and she didn't know if she could stand all that business about the Pope and the BVM. Not that she didn't believe in God, but there was something queer about having an old geezer over in Italy— probably couldn't even speak English either—telling them what they could and couldn't do. Maybe she'd better not suggest anything to Cynthia just yet. Invite her around one evening and see what happens. No good getting tied up with somebody she wouldn't get on with. With a start she realized that the indicator above the door was pointing to M, so she unlocked the door and got in, pressed the button for the third floor, got out and proceeded down the hall toward a heavy door marked "88." Selecting another key from the collection which jangled around her ample waist (or where her waist would have been if she'd had one), she carefully unlocked the heavy door and listened as it closed behind her with a satisfied click.

Caught like a rat in a trap. Trapped like a caught rat. Mrs. Marsden struggled feebly—felt the soft hairs sprout like spring grass upon her body—felt her teeth grow long and pointed, felt her eyes grow small and sharp. She should have known the cheese was tainted—hadn't it been full of holes? She picked up the remains of the cheese in her small sharp claws and stared through the hole, but she could see nothing except the cruel teeth of the trap. The trap grinned at her suddenly and she screamed—but it came out as a squeak, and before she could scamper away the teeth snapped down and click, click bit her in two. Her tail twitched for a moment and then she was still.

Nurse Primrose heard the click, popped her head around the corner of the staff room, where it floated for a minute like a balloon, the features under the starched white cap as colourful and meaningless as the features—painted eyebrows, painted mouth, circles of rouge, stiff glued blond curls—of a child's doll; like a balloon it disappeared. "It's all right," she said, lighting another cigarette, "it's only Mother B." The hawk-faced night nurse finished her coffee in one gulp, took the mug over to the sink and rinsed it carefully, leaving a damp ring of moisture on the table. She dried the cup on a towel marked "88" in indelible ink and put it back on the shelf above the sink, lining it up precisely with the row of green glass mugs already there, each one initialed in nail polish. Then she yawned widely, showing her gold teeth, and picked up her coat and bag.

"See you tomorrow," she said to Nurse Primrose as she went out the door and down the long hall, past the Negro trusty who was busy washing the floor with savage strokes and muttering curses under her breath. The night nurse stepped daintily along the slippery aquarium-coloured linoleum, peering in two of the side wards as she passed. "Jesus," she said to herself. "Why the hell can't they sleep in the night-time?" She nodded curtly to Mother Brown as she passed, but Mother Brown, still lost in the warmth of Florida sunshine and desirable waterfront residences, barely noticed the other woman. Two sets of wet tracks, the night nurse going out and Mother Brown coming in, ran parallel but in opposite directions the length of the long green hall. The trusty looked at the tracks and cursed them musically in a strange, excited tongue. Then she took her wet mop and danced slowly up the hall and back erasing the tracks and laughing to herself at some hidden, apocalyptic joke.

"You miss all the fun," said Nurse Primrose with what she took to be a wry expression.

"What's happened?" Ladling two spoonfuls of Instant Maxwell House into her mug, Mother Brown poured boiling water from the electric kettle and helped herself to several lumps of sugar from the flowered bowl. She sat heavily and gratefully, warming her hands against the mug, and waited. Nurse Primrose wasn't high hat like that other one, thought Mother Brown. Always let you have a cup of coffee before beginning work and didn't put on airs because she had a white cap with a couple of bands and you were only a PN. Nurse Primrose was all right. Pretty, too, with her yellow hair and trim figure. Wonder why she doesn't marry again. Still—once bitten twice shy, and the other one had certainly been a rotter—walking out on her just because she had an abortion and didn't tell him. Why should she have children if she didn't want them, and she had said that with the world in such a dreadful state, it really wasn't right. Mother Brown, no fool, had agreed verbally with the last part of the argument, but had thought of Nurse Primrose's trim figure and the memory of her own confinements, had smiled a little knowing smile to herself. Still Nurse P. was all right. She took a cautious sip of the coffee, singed her tongue. "What's happened?" Nurse Primrose lit another cigarette from the butt she held in her long white fingers.

"Well, I only came on at five of course, so I didn't see or hear it all, but apparently some of the Shocks on 92 got loose—you know the insulin didn't come up on yesterday's plane?" (Mother Brown hadn't known, but she nodded anyway.) "And they tied up Nurse Little and locked her in a closet. Then they went around smashing and screaming until Hilda," (this was the hawk-faced nurse who had nodded to Mother Brown as she went out) "heard the racket and called the Director. It took ten men from the male wards to calm everything down and Mrs. Little has resigned. Had hysterics when they let her out and she's under sedation at her sister's." Her voice dropped to a frightened and delighted whisper. "You see, they couldn't find her at first, what with her being bound and gagged and locked in the broom cupboard, and she had to lie there listening to all the noise and feet and they kept yelling they'd kill her, but they'd dropped the keys somewhere and couldn't get at her—the Shocks I mean. And then the door had to be broken down before they got her out."

The smell and sound of a steam table came rolling down the hall and Nurse Primrose ballooned her head out at the end of the sentence. "Just leave it at the end of the hall— we'll be there in a minute." She popped back in.

"Mark my words," she said in a soft, satisfied voice, "there'll be hell to pay and probably a lot of State Inspectors down from Albany. If Beatrice Little hadn't resigned. . . ." She left the sentence hanging in the smoky air as she adjusted her cap and washed her hands at the sink. Mother Brown ruminated, digesting the news slowly and carefully, her coffee forgotten. "But how did they get loose in the first place?" she ventured, not quite sure of her ground. After all, these nurses stick together. Kind of a union, you might say.

"Exactly," replied Nurse Primrose, crackling out of the room in a flash of starched skirts and yellow hair. "Somebody—naming no names—slipped up."

Thirty-two women, two and thirty ladies, twenty plus twelve creatures on whom the labels lady, woman, person hang uneasily, sniffed the hot steam and recorded the fact, for they cannot be said to have known anything—day or night, sunrise or evening star, Monday or Friday, winter or spring—that they were about to be fed. The continual muttering in the long ward grew louder, rumbled like a vast stomach as the orderly casually ladled porridge into plastic bowls, tea with milk and sugar into plastic cups, stacked up in small towers the toast that had been made three hours before and margarined hastily before dawn. Had anyone wished for an alternate menu, for tea without milk, with milk but without sugar, with lemon perhaps, or toast without "butter," how in the vast web of their verbal confusion could they have found the right words, and would anything have been changed? Porridge and tea and toast with margarine, vitamins in fluted paper cups. After all, it was nourishing—and there were always scrambled eggs (made from powder kept in huge tins in the kitchens) on Sundays. Could they tell it was Sunday by the scrambled eggs? Could they orient themselves in any way by the different palatal sensation (if there is one) between porridge and scrambled powdered eggs? Nurse Primrose and Mother Brown, each starting at one end of the room, coaxed, wheedled, pushed, shoved, threw the food in the thirty-two mouths, or thirty-one, for Mrs. Marsden in spite of the coaxing, wheedling; in spite of firmness which bordered on physical violence, lay still as a stone, her body rigid under the thin blanket, her hands turned up with the fingers curled like claws. Only the faint pulse at her temple indicated that she was alive and listening. Nurse Primrose smacked her playfully on the cheek. "Little girls that don't eat, won't grow up to be big and strong." Nurse Primrose pried open the thin mouth with her crowbar fingers. Mrs. Marsden bit her. Hard.

Rose cried out, but someone smacked away the scream and no sound came. She ran terrified around a room with no corners, a bare room with no cupboards to hide in, no windows and no door. The man ran after her, clumsily, drunkenly. She dared not turn her head but she could hear the heavy thump, thump of his boots upon the floor and smell the hot whisky breath of his coming. Round and round they ran and the room grew smaller and smaller until there was no room, no room to run, no room in the roomless room. He jerked her to him, flung himself upon her, pressed her against the wall. She could feel his hot metallic mouth upon her face, his tongue thrusting against her teeth. "Rape," she cried frantically—but no sound came and as she opened her mouth his tongue forced its way in and his hot saliva dribbled down her chin. "Well, there's one that'll always open up," said Mother Brown with satisfaction as she moved off down the ward.

An orderly came in to help them make the beds. Together with Aunt Jemima, the Negro trusty, the four of them paired off and worked quickly (roll the patient over, swab the rubber sheet, put on the draw sheet with a quick pull, rolling the body to the other side, plump the pillows, arrange the coarse muslin nightgown—everything stamped with "88" to make sure nothing was lost or sent to the wrong place—the blanket drawn up, the body tucked in and folded precisely, as though it were an important letter— order out of chaos). The nurses retired for a break while

Aunt Jemima, her hooded eyes revealing nothing, immersed in her own particular dream, chuckled musically to herself and began cleaning filth off the iron-grey beds.

Mother Brown plugged in the electric kettle, and Nurse Primrose lit a cigarette. "I don't know," she said thoughtfully, looking at her bandaged finger. "Sometimes I wonder why I don't ask for a transfer. They think we have it easy up here—all these dear little old ladies and all in bed—but I'm sick of the smell of shit," (Mother Brown winced inwardly. She always referred to it as "Number Two") "and bed sores and trying to jolly up a lot of vegetables." She stared at her finger. "Sometimes I think I'd like to quit the whole deal and get married again, but I suppose that's the same thing really—work your fingers to the bone—except you don't get paid for it."

Mother Brown clucked sympathetically. "What you need, my dear, is a holiday or a little trip. A change is as good as a rest they always say." She wondered if she should show Nurse Primrose the brochures, take her mind off her troubles—probably just her period—what's she got to worry about on her pay and at her age? She decided against it and sipped her coffee in what she hoped was a sympathetic manner.

Nurse Primrose patted her yellow curls and blew a smoke ring. "I suppose that's it. Of course it's really the responsibility that cripples me. All this book work, signing for drugs, check and double check, and those bitches from the Grey Ladies waltzing in every week with their crap about 'brightening up a dreary life' and 'musical afternoons' and that kook doctor hanging around with his 'while there's life there's hope' jazz. Sometimes," she said, looking at Mother Brown with her doll-baby eyes, "I envy you PNs. *You're* not responsible if one of the old dears falls out of bed and breaks her hip. *You* don't have to talk to the relatives if one of them kicks the bucket. I wouldn't be surprised," she said spitefully, "if that PN on 92, what's-her-name, your friend—didn't have something to do with all the hoo-hah last night. Didn't tie 'em down tight enough or something. But *she* didn't get locked in the cupboard—oh no!"

Feathers ruffling, Mother Brown said icily, "My *acquaintance*—" she underlined the word with the tip of her pink tongue "—my acquaintance, Cynthia Goodwood, to whom I've no doubt you refer, is a highly trained practical nurse. I'm quite sure she. . ."

"Forget it," said Nurse Primrose. "I was only being bitchy." Mother Brown accepted the apology with a hurt nod of her head, but their relationship was cool for the rest of the day.

Eleanor La Douce danced the shimmy in New Orleans with a sailor named Joe. Eleanor, the sweet young thing, danced the shimmy on Canal Street with a sailor named Tom, a sailor named Dick, and Harry the drummer who sold ladies' lingerie and told her tales of tall mountains in the West and tall tales of buildings in New York. Eleanor shimmied and shook with longing. Eleanor strutted and stuck her little bottom out. "Gimme a break, sister," said Harry, Tom and Dick. "My last night in port," whispered the sailor whose name she had forgotten. "How much you willing to pay?" said Eleanor, and she and Tom and she and Dick and she and Harry and the sailor shimmied across the floor and through the beaded curtain at the rear. "Has it come to this?" shrieked Eleanor La Douce, as she rummaged in her pillow-case with frantic hands. "You have stolen my jewels, my château on the Loire, my baby with the raven curls. Whores, villains, hags and harpies." She spat a mouthful of feathers into the air where they floated dreamily onto the green floor.

You are wrong, you philosophers, we are not the sum of

all our yesterdays, but the product of all the tomorrows which never came. Wrapped in our dreams we only wake to yesterday and madness and damnation.

Mother Brown, somewhat surprised at her boldness, announced, and did not ask, that she would take her lunch at 11.30. The idea of the cold walk across the compound made her wish she had packed a lunch, but, hugging her black plastic bag full of Florida oranges and palm trees and a pleasant breeze from the sea, she ventured forth, the cruel wind waiting for her just outside the door. Head down, she waddled briskly toward the canteen. Cynthia was already there, her little finger crooked daintily around a chipped and flowered teacup. Mother Brown picked up a plastic tray and took her place in line.

"I suppose you've heard about last night?" asked Cynthia, taking a dainty sip of tea. "Yes," replied Mother Brown rather curtly, her mind on other things. She attacked her stew, chewing the meat with difficulty and pleasure. The warm food made her feel more cheerful, and as she pushed her plate to one side and began on the cottage pudding, she smiled at Cynthia, whose voice had been tinkling away for some time.

"Well, it's nothing to smile about, my dear. You wouldn't have liked it to have happened to you."

"But it didn't happen to you, did it?" The words came out muffled in crumbs and custard.

"It didn't, but it might have. I tell you, I've been feeling *queer* all day, and could only take tea and toast for lunch." She looked accusingly at her friend's tray. Dropping her voice to a whisper, she leaned across the scarred table to Mother Brown, squeezing her words out carefully, like toothpaste.

"You-know-who asked me to work the night shift yesterday, but I said, 'No thank you, dearie, not I, I have social

171

commitments this evening and cannot possibly get back here by midnight.' " Cynthia was fond of her social commitments, although their nature had not as yet been revealed to her new friend. " 'I realize,' I said, 'that I am relatively new here, and only a lowly PN, but the Goodwoods are not used to being pushed around. The Goodwoods,' I said to her, 'practically own the bank in East Orange, New Jersey.' " Believing, by now, that she really had said all this, her thin face was flushed with righteous indignation. "And if I had *stayed* —!" She gave a delicate shudder. "I feel a migraine," (she pronounced it mee-grain) "coming on. I know I shall have a sick headache by tonight, just *thinking* about it. Perhaps," she said tentatively, "I should do what George and Eunice have been begging me to do all along and move in with them." She looked as though she might cry. Mother Brown seized her opportunity. "What would you think," she offered tentatively, "of coming to Florida or California with me? A few more months and I should have enough to put a down payment on a cottage, and with Harry's pension and my social security I think I'll have enough to live on. Naturally both kids want me to live with them when I quit, but I think young people should be by themselves, don't you?"

"Oh, I *agree*," replied Mrs. Goodwood thoughtfully, as she turned the idea around, examining it for flaws as one might examine a ripe peach or a cantaloupe. One could almost see her picking it up and smelling it. "But Florida—I don't know. So many Jews down there, aren't there, and of course there are my social commitments to consider. And the children would be *devastated*, if their Mama went so far away."

Mother Brown patted her bag, then glanced at the clock. "Well, you think it over. I've got some lovely brochures from different places—but of course I can always find someone else. I just thought, seeing as how you don't like it here very much, and with your husband having passed over, you might feel a bit lonely and at loose ends."

"Oh I'm never *lonely*," interjected Cynthia with a tinkling laugh suggestive of too many, rather than too few, acquaintances. "Still, it might be nice. A change and all that. This climate is certainly bad for my sinus. The doctors' bills I've had to pay for drainage!"

"I'll tell you what," said Mother Brown casually, picking up her coat and adjusting her galoshes, "why don't you come around to my place some night and we'll have a cup of tea and a chat about it. That is, if your social commitments would allow it." Cynthia glanced sharply at her friend's face, but Mother Brown was the picture of innocence as she fastened her plastic rain scarf over her cap.

"Well, I *couldn't* get away this evening, but perhaps tomorrow night?" Mother Brown left her two of the most attractive brochures and her address as they parted at the elevator. The aluminum Christmas tree, exotic and immortal, shimmered gaily in the hall. But Mother Brown was again lost beneath the palms and failed to give it the attention it deserved.

A male nurse, virginal yet virile in his white uniform, travelled downward, passing Mother Brown between the third and second floors. In one hand he carried a large tin can, under his arm a crudely wrapped brown-paper parcel. He hated working in the OR at any time, but this morning had been terrible. The two doctors, like second-rate comedians, with their endless stories of the golf club. And that kike doctor, Weinstein, was the end, with his bit about the daughter and her private dance. Think they're pretty cool—donate their time and collect it back on the income tax. Charity. Services for one amputation and one. . . . Usual fee. What would the usual fee amount to? Something in three figures anyway. Not nice to think about, though, all that chopping off of this and that. The RCs have to keep it all, I think. Can't stand up at Judgment Day if so much as a toe is missing. Still (he brightened), he'd drop these off on his way over to lunch. That fat-assed bitch in pathology would have a treat. "Listen, sweetheart," he'd say to her, "which would you rather have, the drumstick or the breast?" Whistling, he got out.

Dinner consists of minced spam and mashed potatoes, custard-powder custard—and tea with milk. Everything minced and mashed, chopped and creamed to facilitate its easy mastication by tired or toothless jaws. Equality and custard-powder custard for all. Mother Brown and the orderly move efficiently up and down the rows. Thirty-two old ladies in rows of eight. But one extra bowl, for Mother Brown, taking no chances, never pauses by the bed of Mrs. Marsden. Aunt Jemima scoops up the extra dinner with her fingers, squatting on her haunches in the corner. "White trash," she mutters, "goddamned white trash." But whether this referred to the food or something else she does not say. Steam trolley rolls off on its rubber-soled feet and Nurse Primrose returns, flushed and pretty from the cold, to give the afternoon sedation. Then the recreation room is tidied, although it is never used on 88. Visitors' Day, and you never know who might peek in. On one wall of the room is a reproduction of Van Gogh's *Starry Night*; across from it a dusty print, slightly out of focus, of a young girl with a muff. The walls are the colour of milky tea and porridge, a colour not recommended by the best interior decorators, but cheap and serviceable, the colour of No-Hope and muddy rivers. An empathetic colour and perhaps more suitable than the state would understand or realize. There are a few benches running along the walls, as though an amateur performance might be about to begin, and one or two sofas with sagging springs covered with faded chintz. Here the potted plants will be placed at night, and the cut flowers, pushed anyhow into jam jars or the occasional, donated, vase, will wither and fade in the damp, overheated air. The flowers and plants sometimes would be returned to the ward the next morning or, more often than not, would stand neglected and unnoticed until the next Visitors' Day (Monday Wednesday Friday four to five and by special permission of the Director in cases of extreme emergency). Unnoticed, except by an old Negro woman, who would shuffle in when no-one was looking and reach out tentative and trembling hands toward the blooming memory of warmth and colour and long ago. Recreation room—but why should we be concerned with recreation in the case of thirty-two old ladies? They would neither understand nor appreciate. Better left in their beds, where they can bloom like hothouse flowers amid their fantasies of past and future. Mother Brown closed the door behind her as she went out.

The visitors leaked in, not very many, for the weather was cold. Not very many ever, for the ladies were old. They deposited their offerings at the Staff Room and went shyly and slowly into the ward. What, after all, does one say to a crumpled face, a blank or furious stare? "Hello, Mother. Well, here we are again. Everything all right? Can you hear me, Mother? Are they treating you well? She looks well, doesn't she, Dad?" Conversation trickles off into little drops of "hem" and "well, well, well." How does one converse with madness? For the sane it is impossible, and the insane do not care about each other. "Well, I think she knew we were there," they say hesitantly to Nurse Primrose as they shrug their way back down the hall. "You'll tell her we came, won't you?" "Certainly," replies the painted and professional smile. "I'm sure she appreciates your visit." She hurries them along with her cheerful, clattering chatter. The occasional priest or minister. The occasional minister's wife. "Come unto me all ye that labour and are heavy laden. . . ." A few prayers—a feeling of having done all one can. Perhaps a word of remembrance after the Sunday sermon. Mentioning no names of course. "Whew," says Nurse Primrose, lighting her cigarette, "I'm glad that's over." The wet shoes and boots have left puddles of melted snow along the rows and down the corridor. She frowns at this disorder.

Mother Brown took off her galoshes and stood them carefully on the classified section of yesterday's paper. She changed her stockings and turned up the thermostat. Waddling across the doily-covered room in her carpet slippers, she went into the little kitchen, lit the gas under the kettle, and took a package of birdseed from the pantry shelf. Carefully she opened the cage, and the little bird, head on one side, peered at her inquisitively and hopped out onto her thick finger. "There's a good boy," she said, and with her free hand she drew out the soiled paper and the empty cup. "Did you miss me?" she crooned, admiring his pretty feathers and bright eyes. The bird flew over to the mantelpiece and perched below a faded picture of a young woman and man on their wedding day. The woman was plump and coyly smiling. The man was thin, and not much taller than his partner. He looked as though something had disagreed with him. Holding a silver paper horseshoe, they stared fixedly at Mother Brown as she cleaned the cage and put fresh water in the little cup. "What do you think, Petey?" she said lovingly, "I've brought you a present." And from her handbag she produced a little mirror which she hung by a string from the top of the cage. She put the bird back gently, fastened the door, and sat down with a cup of tea before the television set. She wondered sleepily, before the sound came on, if Cynthia had a canary. "The children will be devastated!" Still, Cynthia *was* refined and it would cut down on the mortgage. She supposed Cynthia would want the property under a joint name. Well, they'd have to see about that. Wonder if Cynthia has an account of her own. Must find everything out. Wouldn't do to get mixed up with her unless the whole thing was clear. The picture on the television screen attracted her attention and she forgot Cynthia in the excitement of her program.

Eleanor La Douce, her fingers busy, quickly and gleefully braided strips of bed sheet into a long, firm plait. The night nurse dozed over her *True Confessions* as Eleanor scrambled out of the room, her nightshirt flapping crazily around her skinny legs. She climbed on top of the washbasin and quickly and efficiently hanged herself from the steel light fixture. Swaying gracefully, as though to an old and lovely melody, Eleanor waltzed slowly toward the waiting arms of General La Douce.

Mother Brown turned heavily once and went back to her cottage. Hands tucked under her fat cheeks, she dreamed of oranges and slept the sleep of the just.